IT WATCHES IN THE DARK

IT WATCHES IN THE DARK

JEFF STRAND

EEK!

sourcebooks
young readers

Published by Sourcebooks Young Readers, an imprint of Sourcebooks
P.O. Box 4410, Naperville, Illinois 60567-4410
(630) 961-3900
sourcebooks.com

Cataloging-in-Publication Data is on file with the Library of Congress.

This product conforms to all applicable CPSC and CPSIA standards.

Source of Production: LSC Communications, Harrisonburg, Virginia, USA
Date of Production: January 2024
Tradepaper ISBN: 9781728277622. Run Number: 5020082
Hardcover ISBN: 9781728277592. Run Number 5030078

Printed and bound in the United States of America.
LSC 10 9 8 7 6 5 4 3 2 1

*Dedicated to everybody who
likes things spooooooooky!*

CHAPTER ONE

"Hold on," said Dad. "It's gonna get a bit rough."

Oliver adjusted his life vest, even though it was perfectly snug already. He held on to his seat in the middle of the canoe with both hands. He wasn't scared—not yet—but those rapids up ahead looked worse than anything they'd anticipated on this trip.

"Do you want to trade places?" he asked Trisha, who sat in front of him. He hoped she'd say no.

His twin sister glanced back at him and smiled. "Nope, I'm fine."

Oliver breathed a sigh of relief.

Dad sat in the back, so he was responsible for steering.

For most of the trip, he'd relaxed in the center seat, letting Oliver and Trisha paddle and steer. They were good at it— they spent every other weekend with Dad, and these weekends almost always involved some time on the water.

"Everybody down," said Dad.

Oliver and Trisha knelt on the bottom of the canoe. This was to lower their center of gravity and make it less likely that the canoe would tip over in the rough water. Dad didn't sound worried, so Oliver decided he wouldn't worry either. Everything would be fine. The violently churning water up ahead was no big deal.

"It'll be okay," Dad assured them. "Worst-case scenario, our stuff gets wet."

Of course, there were many scenarios worse than water getting into the canoe. They could lose their gear. Or get dragged along the rocky river bottom by the current. Or eaten by a great white shark that had gotten lost. Or, you know, *drown*. Even if you stuck to the plausible scenarios, there were many, many, many things worse than spending the night in a damp sleeping bag.

Oliver hoped Trisha was too busy paddling to glance back at him because he was sure he looked frightened. Not that she'd make fun of him, but still...

Trisha glanced back. "Don't be scared."

"I'm not," he insisted.

"We'll be fine."

"I know."

And they would be. Dad wouldn't have taken them on this adventure if they weren't ready. Mom would never have allowed it. It was slightly rougher water than they'd anticipated, sure, but they'd be through it quickly, and the knot in Oliver's stomach would disappear. Then they could eat lunch.

Even if Dad wasn't there, Oliver and Trisha would've been fine. They worked well together in a canoe. Most people would say, "Well, of course! They're twins!" But Oliver and Trisha got on each other's nerves more often than they finished each other's sentences. They didn't share a secret language or feel pain when the other one stubbed their toe, or anything like that. Being in sync while paddling the canoe came from hours and hours of practice, not any kind of psychic twin bond.

They didn't have many common interests either. Oliver was into books and video games, while Trisha was into sports and more sports. Still, they both loved being out on the water with their father.

Dad hadn't stopped grinning since he'd picked them up. Actually, he hadn't stopped grinning since Mom had (reluctantly) given him permission to take them on a five-day trip down the Champion River for their twelfth birthday. And the trip, now in the early afternoon of its third day, was going great. Sleeping in a tent every night! Campfires! Ghost stories! S'mores!

When they got home, they'd have the usual "birthday cake and presents" party with their friends, but it wouldn't be nearly as much fun.

"Listen for my instructions," said Dad, raising his voice over the rushing water.

And then they were in the rapids.

It was like being on a wet roller coaster. Water sprayed Oliver's face, getting in his eyes. At least it wasn't salt water. He blinked the water out.

"Paddle hard!" Dad shouted over the roar of the river.

Oliver held his breath, his grip tightening on the seat. A quick turn, and they narrowly missed a tree branch that jutted into the river.

Another quick maneuver, and they navigated between some large rocks, picking up speed as they went.

Everyone in the boat was focused. They were almost

through the worst of it. It was going to be totally fine. A few more yards and—

The canoe jolted as if the Loch Ness Monster had risen beneath it. But it wasn't Nessie—they'd struck a huge rock.

The canoe spun.

Then it flipped.

Oliver had been splashed by the water constantly during this trip and even sometimes trailed his hand in the river, but he wasn't prepared for just how *cold* it felt to plunge into it.

In some places, the Champion River was over his head, and in some places, it wasn't. He gripped his life jacket and frantically kicked his feet, hoping to touch the bottom. He couldn't. He was carried off with the current, followed by the overturned canoe.

He looked around, trying not to panic. They'd practiced what to do if they capsized, but he couldn't see Trisha or Dad.

"Oliver!" Trisha screamed.

He still couldn't see her, but her voice came from the other side of the canoe. He grabbed for it and missed.

Oliver spat out some water. "I'm okay!"

Where was Dad?

Oliver tried to grab the canoe and missed again. It slid ahead of him, and he saw Trisha desperately holding on to the other side.

There was no sign of Dad. They were all wearing bright orange life jackets, but Oliver couldn't see one bobbing in the water around him. Was Dad submerged? Behind them? Dad could be anywhere.

How long had it been? Twenty seconds? Dad could hold his breath for twenty seconds, no problem.

Oliver's shoes scraped along the river bottom. He tried to stop his forward momentum, but the water was still too fast and too deep.

Trisha and the canoe were getting farther and farther away.

Oliver tried to scream for their father but got a mouthful of cold water. He coughed and sputtered, then scanned the river again.

There! He caught a glimpse of orange in the water!

It was about ten feet behind him. Though Oliver was floating down the middle of the river, Dad (that *had* to be Dad!) was much closer to the edge.

Oliver couldn't see the orange anymore.

No! There it was! Dad bobbed to the surface. But it wasn't

Dad smiling and waving at him. He was facedown, letting the river's current carry him along.

Oliver swam toward him. He wasn't super athletic, and swimming across the current would be a challenge for anybody, but he had to do this!

He felt like his arms were on fire, even in the freezing water, but he pushed harder.

He was getting closer. Closer.

Closer...

He grabbed Dad by the vest. Oliver tried to turn him over, to get his face out of the water, but it was difficult enough to hold on to him.

"Oliver!"

He looked over at Trisha. She'd righted the canoe, run it up the riverbank, and was holding out her paddle. If he missed it, he and Dad would be swept along the river for who knew how long.

Trisha waded into the river, extending the paddle.

Clinging to Dad's vest, Oliver reached for it.

Got it!

He pulled Dad onto his back, but his life jacket was slipping out of Oliver's grasp. He couldn't lose him now!

The paddle slid out of Oliver's numb fingers, and the

two were swept forward. Oliver tried to dig his feet into the dirt and rocks of the riverbed to slow them down. It wasn't working.

Oliver didn't give up. He could do this. He knew he could do this. He was *not* going to let go of Dad. They were *not* going to be carried down the river to their doom.

And then, not too far past Trisha, it started to work. The water was smoother and not as deep. They both slowed, giving Oliver a chance to breathe.

He wanted to say something reassuring, but his teeth were chattering too much for him to speak. He dragged Dad to the edge of the river, where Trisha hurried over to meet them. Together they pulled their father out of the water.

Dad slumped over to the side. His eyes were closed. Water spilled down his face, and then it turned red.

"Is he okay?" Oliver asked, barely able to get out the words. "Is he breathing?"

"I—I think so? I can't tell!" Trisha pressed her fingers into Dad's wrist. "I think he has a pulse."

"You *think*?"

"He's freezing, and my hands are freezing!" She waited a moment. "Okay, there's definitely a pulse. And he's breathing."

Oliver was so relieved that he wanted to burst into tears.

"Go get the first aid kit from the canoe," said Trisha.

Normally, Oliver didn't like being ordered around by his sister, but she was absolutely right. He ran over to the canoe. The first aid kit had been strapped down, so he unfastened and grabbed it, then ran back to Trisha and Dad.

"Thanks," said Trisha, opening it.

As she took out some gauze, Oliver pulled his cell phone out of his pocket and removed it from the protective bag. They were deep in the wilderness, and it was possible there was no signal out here, but he'd hope for the best.

He turned on the phone and waited a few excruciating moments for it to power up. When it did, he had no bars.

"I'm going to see if I can find a signal," he told Trisha. She nodded, focused on their father.

Shivering, Oliver walked along the riverbank, holding the phone up in the air as if getting it three feet higher might make the difference. Both sides of the river were thick forest—clearly nobody lived around here. Wandering through the woods in the hope of stumbling upon help would be a useless effort.

He kept walking while Trisha patched up Dad's head wound, but he hurried back when she called out that she was finished.

"Anything?" she asked.

Oliver shook his head. "How bad was it?"

"It wasn't *good*," said Trisha. "But I think he'll be okay. We need to get him to a doctor as soon as possible."

"Let's get him in the canoe and keep going down the river. If we don't find a phone signal, we'll at least see a house or cabin." It had been a while since they'd passed one, but it wasn't as if they were deep in a remote area of the Amazon. They were in Missouri. If they kept floating down the river, they'd come across someone before too long.

Fortunately, it wasn't that difficult to maneuver Dad into the canoe, even while needing to be extremely careful. Oliver was nobody's idea of a super athlete, but he could help lift Dad without accidentally dropping him.

Trisha, meanwhile, *was* a super athlete. Also, she'd begun her growth spurt. Oliver wasn't a big fan of being three inches shorter than his twin sister, but he'd catch up eventually.

"It's going to be fine, Dad," said Trisha. "We'll find help, I promise."

Dad did not respond.

They resumed the trip, though it was no longer any fun. Oliver's heart was racing as much as it had in the rapids.

"He'll be fine," Trisha told Oliver. "I bet he'll wake up soon."

"His head was bleeding pretty bad. And what if he gets hypothermia?"

"It looked worse than it really was. We'll probably have to stop him from grabbing a paddle. He'll want to make up for the time we lost."

Oliver didn't like that his sister—who was technically thirteen minutes younger—was trying to hide the reality of their situation from him as if he were a little kid. Or maybe she was trying to hide it from herself.

As they paddled down the river, Oliver kept an eye on his cell phone, waiting for a mere one bar to show up on the display. Enough for emergency services to track their location and send a helicopter. Not that there was anywhere to land a helicopter—they'd probably have to lower a stretcher on a rope to whisk him away.

What if they didn't find anybody before nightfall? What if Dad stayed unconscious? It would be too dangerous to canoe down the river after dark. He needed medical attention now.

Dad let out a soft moan but didn't open his eyes.

Trisha's back was to Oliver, but he heard her sniffle. Oliver couldn't think of anything reassuring to say.

They didn't speak for a while. Oliver was suddenly struck by the fear that there might be even worse rapids ahead, rapids that would catapult Dad right out of the canoe.

Stop that, he told himself. *Focus on the immediate problem.*

They continued down the river. Adrenaline coursed through Oliver's body, but his arms were getting tired. Where were the people? Where were the other boats? Oliver wanted to scream at his phone to find a signal, but that wouldn't do any good, and he didn't want Trisha to think he couldn't handle a crisis. If she could stay calm, so could he.

He kept checking on Dad, making sure he was still breathing. Why wouldn't he wake up? If he had an internet connection, Oliver could google how long it took somebody to regain consciousness after they'd been knocked out.

"There!" Trisha shouted as Oliver saw it himself. A large wooden dock! Though it wasn't in the best shape, it didn't look completely abandoned. There was a rowboat tied there. A rowboat wasn't nearly as useful as a speedboat, but it showed that somebody was actually using the dock.

A trail led into the trees. Maybe there was a cabin out of view.

A cabin didn't mean there'd be anybody inside to help, but at least this was *something*.

They paddled the canoe until it gently bumped against the dock. Trisha got out.

"You stay with Dad," she said. "I'll see if I can find somebody."

"No. We'll both go."

"We can't leave him alone."

"Why not?" Oliver asked. "Nobody's going to kidnap him. I'm not going to let you walk through the woods alone."

He didn't like seeing all the cobwebs in the rowboat. It was a pretty clear sign nobody had used it recently, but he wasn't going to point that out.

Trisha was also looking into the rowboat, and he wondered if she'd come to the same conclusion. "What if somebody comes down the river while we're gone and we miss them?"

"Dad's unconscious in a canoe with his head all bandaged. They'll stop to see what's wrong. You're not going by yourself. I'm not debating it."

"All right," said Trisha. "But let's hurry."

Oliver got out of the canoe, and they slid it up on shore, then firmly tied it to the dock. Dad wasn't going anywhere.

"Everything's going to be all right," he said to Dad before hurrying up the trail with Trisha. Oliver only wished he believed it.

CHAPTER TWO

Trisha thought she'd been doing a good job hiding how scared she was. Dad desperately needed medical attention, and if they were walking down a long trail that led to an abandoned cabin, they'd be wasting time they simply did not have.

They'd been hurrying along the trail for about five minutes, moving fast but not fast enough to trip on the uneven ground. The last thing they needed was a sprained ankle. So far there was only forest, with absolutely no sign that anybody lived out here. They had to keep going, at least a little farther, but the truth was the trail probably didn't lead anywhere helpful.

"When do we give up?" she asked.

"What? We don't!"

"I don't mean give up on Dad. I mean give up on this trail."

"Why would we give up on the trail?"

"If we *do* find a cabin, and somebody *is* there, that doesn't mean they can help us. Their cell phone won't get a signal either."

"Maybe they have a landline or one of those military phones," said Oliver. "Or maybe this trail leads to a road, with cars and stuff."

"It might," said Trisha. "It totally could. But the farther we go, the longer it is to get back, and at some point, we're going to have to decide if we're taking too much of a risk."

"The trail is in good shape," Oliver offered. "I mean, there aren't fresh footprints or anything, but it's not overgrown. It has to lead somewhere, right?"

"I'm not talking about the trail becoming a dead end. I'm saying that if we walk a few miles and it ends at an empty cabin, we've cost ourselves a lot of time that Dad might not have. And maybe there are people farther downriver."

"Five more minutes," said Oliver.

"Okay."

About four minutes later, almost all at once, the trail opened into a large clearing.

Not simply a clearing. A whole town.

The dirt trail became a cobblestone street, with small houses on each side. A sign read ESCROW. POPULATION 999. Escrow? Wasn't that a money term? Trisha wasn't entirely certain what it meant, but she'd heard Mom talking about it when she was buying a house after the divorce. The name didn't matter. Surely with 999 residents, somebody here could help them.

"It's weird that there's a sign here," said Oliver. "How many people visit a town after walking up a trail from a random river dock? Shouldn't they put the sign by the river so people know it's here?"

It did seem weird, but they had more important things to worry about.

The houses looked old. Not like they'd been built a long time ago—if anything, they were new, all freshly painted and in very good condition. It was more like they were built in the style of old homes, reminding Trisha of the time they'd gone on a tour of a colonial town. She could imagine Benjamin Franklin or somebody like that living here.

There seemed to be several rows of houses laid out in straight lines.

They hurried to the closest house. A welcome mat said simply HELLO. There was no doorbell, so Trisha knocked.

A moment later, the curtain in the front window shifted, as if somebody was peeking out. Then the door opened.

A tall heavyset man with a thick gray beard stood in the doorway. Trisha had half expected to see somebody in 1700s garb with a tricornered hat, but the man was wearing blue jeans and a white T-shirt. He looked very surprised to see them. "Oh, hi," he said, raising an eyebrow. "May I...help you?"

"Sorry to bother you," said Trisha. "We were on a canoe trip, and our dad got injured. We need help."

"Oh, wow, yeah, okay," said the man, stepping out of his house. "Don't worry, I'm not going to hurt you."

"I—I didn't think you were," Trisha stammered, suddenly wondering if they should trust this stranger. But maybe he thought they looked scared of him. And what choice did they have but to follow him?

The man shut the door behind him. "We're going this way." He began to walk down the street. "It's not far. It's not far at all. All is well."

Trisha and Oliver exchanged concerned glances, but they followed him. Trisha wished he would walk a bit faster, but if the man was going to help them, she wasn't going to tell him to pick up the pace.

"Almost there," said the man as they passed a few homes. "Almost there, I promise. See? Right there. Just like I told you."

He walked up to a house that didn't look any different from the other houses on the street. He pounded on the door with his right hand. When no one answered after a few seconds, he pounded on the door with both hands, and then he pounded a catchy rhythm. A moment later, the door opened. A woman poked her head out. Her hair was pulled back in a tight ponytail, and she wore thick glasses with red frames.

"Jeez, Frank, are you trying to break down my—?" She noticed the twins. "Oh, hello."

"They need help," said Frank.

"Sorry to bother you," said Trisha. "Our dad had an accident on the river and hurt his head. He's unconscious. We left him down by the dock."

"Well, why didn't you say something?" asked the woman. It seemed like a strange question, since Trisha thought she'd gotten straight to the point. "We'll get your father. We're a small village, but we have excellent medical services, and we will save him. As long as he *can* be saved, of course."

Trisha and Oliver looked at each other again. Oliver opened his mouth as if about to protest, but Trisha gave a quick shake of her head, and he remained silent.

The woman walked over to a telephone mounted on the wall of her living room. She picked it up and dialed— actually dialed. It was one of those rotary phones Trisha had only seen in old movies, never in real life.

"Hi," the woman said into the receiver. "It's Belinda. We need a team down by the dock. A man has been hurt. Head injury. Unconscious. Thanks." She hung up the phone. "I'm going to meet them at the medical center. Frank, entertain the children until you hear from me."

"We'd like to go with you," Trisha said.

"No. Somebody will let you know as soon as we've retrieved him, and then we'll give you an update on his condition after I've examined him."

"Shouldn't I show you where he is?"

"You said he was at the dock. There's only one dock. Unless he's floated away, it should be easy to find him. With all due respect, you two will be a distraction, and your father will get better care if I'm not distracted." She stepped out of the house and, with a polite nod, walked quickly down the street, leaving them behind.

"Where's the medical center?" Trisha asked Frank.

"It's not too far. Nothing's too far in Escrow." Frank sighed. "Guess I'm supposed to entertain you." He looked at Trisha, then at Oliver. "You like jacks?"

"Excuse me?"

"Jacks. The game. You bounce the ball and then scoop up the jacks before you catch it. The ball doesn't bounce very well on the cobblestone, but we could find another place to play."

Trisha shook her head. "No, we don't want to play a game right now," she said, trying to make sure she didn't sound rude or ungrateful. "We want to make sure our dad is okay."

"Thing is, you won't be the one operating on him. So it doesn't matter if you're playing jacks or not."

"You think he'll need surgery?" Oliver asked, panic creeping into his voice.

Frank shrugged. "I'm not a doctor. It's not up to me to decide. You said he hurt his head, and I don't know if that means he's got a bump on the noggin or if his head is most of the way off."

Trisha wasn't quite sure what to say to that. "I'd really like to go with the medics to get him."

"Hey, you haven't been kidnapped," Frank told her. "If you run, I'm not going to tackle you to the ground. But if you're a distraction, like Belinda said, and your dad dies because of it, how'll that make you feel?"

Trisha said nothing.

"I don't want to play jacks," said Oliver.

"If I'd known you were coming, I would've made a big, long list of activities, but I didn't wake up this morning thinking you'd knock on my door, so you've got to cut me a little slack."

"I'm sorry," said Trisha. "We're worried."

Frank sighed. "I understand. I'd be worried and unpleasant in your situation too." He thought for a moment. "What about cookies? Do you like cookies?"

Trisha looked at Oliver, who shrugged. "We're not very hungry," said Trisha for them both.

Up ahead, Belinda disappeared around the corner.

"Could you take us to the medical center?" Trisha asked. "We won't go inside or get in the way. We just want to see them bring him in."

"Yeah, yeah, I guess that'll be fine," said Frank. "I assume they'll wheel him in on a gurney, so you can't run up to him and start crying because you could knock him onto the ground and hurt his head even more. But it's a nice wide street. You can watch without getting in anybody's way." He walked in the direction Belinda had gone. The twins followed.

"You're brother and sister?" Frank asked.

"Yes," said Oliver. "We're twins."

"Twins? I thought twins looked like two copies of the same kid."

"We're fraternal twins, not identical twins."

"Ah, okay. I learned something new. I guess you never know what any given day has in store, huh?"

"I guess not," said Oliver.

"I mean, I'll bet you didn't wake up this morning thinking you wouldn't know if your dad was going to live or die, did you?" Frank glanced back at them and frowned. "I'm sorry. That was probably insensitive. We don't get outsiders here very often, so we're not good at being considerate about their feelings."

"It's okay," said Trisha.

"If I say something like that again, feel free to tell me, 'Hey, Frank, we'd rather cut off our ears with an axe than listen to you talk.' That'll shut me right up."

Trisha gave Frank a little smile, but she couldn't help worrying he meant it literally.

They walked in silence for about a minute.

"I have a confession," said Frank. "I don't have any jacks. I lost them years ago. I wouldn't even know where to get any. I don't know why I asked if you wanted to play. Sometimes I talk without thinking. I'm glad you didn't want to play because it would've been really awkward."

Neither Trisha nor Oliver responded because they rounded the corner and stopped in place, gaping at what they saw ahead of them.

"Welcome to the village square," said Frank. "This is where we have our meetings and festivals. This place is very important to us. I keep it clean. I mean, a few people do, but I'm one of them."

Trisha didn't care who was responsible for picking up litter. She was too distracted by the giant scarecrow.

It wasn't simply big by the standards of a normal scarecrow—it was the height of a two-story house. It was mounted on a huge wooden pole, with its arms stretched to each side. Its hands were enormous white gloves, with straw protruding from its wrists. It wore a red plaid shirt with blue overalls, and large brown boots, also with straw sticking out of the top. It had a triangular nose, rosy-red cheeks, eyes made from giant buttons, and a stitched mouth with a great big smile.

It looked as if the scarecrow had been part of the village for a long time, as if the houses and buildings had been constructed around it. Yet it didn't look old or worn. It seemed as if the villagers took great pride in caring for it. And for some reason, Trisha couldn't help but feel as if those button eyes were watching her.

It was the wind, of course, but it almost looked like it was...*breathing.*

Except there wasn't any wind.

"Did you see that?" Oliver whispered.

The giant scarecrow was not breathing. That was ridiculous.

"It feels like it's looking at us," said Oliver.

Trisha agreed with him. It *did* feel like the scarecrow was looking at them. Which was equally ridiculous—it had buttons for eyes. No pupils. Nothing to follow them as they moved.

They were freaked out because of Dad, and their minds weren't working as well as they should. This was not a breathing, staring scarecrow. It was a giant piece of burlap stuffed with straw. Nothing more.

Frank smiled. "Impressive, huh? He's very special to us. He keeps us safe."

"Keeps you safe?" Oliver asked.

Frank nodded. "He watches over us. Protects us."

"From what?"

"From whatever might cause us harm," he said in a slow low voice. "From whatever might cause us harm."

Trisha had been so fixated on the scarecrow that she hadn't noticed the dozen stone benches surrounding it. It was weird enough that anybody would want to sit near that thing, but there was seating for a large group. What kind of meetings did they have here? The important meetings at home were held at the town hall or in the high school auditorium.

"Does it...have a name?" Trisha asked.

"Nah," said Frank. "Naming a scarecrow would be silly."

"It's creepy," said Oliver.

Frank scowled at him. "He's not creepy. How would you like it if I came to your village and called your protector creepy?"

Frank was an imposing man and seemed genuinely angry. Trisha found herself taking a step away from him, as if he might do something worse than scowl.

"I'm sorry," said Oliver. "I didn't mean to insult you. I'm just worried about my dad."

"Your fraternal twin sister is also worried about your dad, but you don't hear her calling our scarecrow *creepy*, do you? Are you a coward, kid? What's your name?"

"Oliver."

"Are you a coward, Oliver?" he asked, his voice quavering in rage.

"No, sir."

"Farmers put up scarecrows all the time. If you saw a scarecrow in a cornfield, would you run and hide in the truck? Would they find you in the back seat crying your little eyes out?"

"He said he was sorry," said Trisha.

"I heard him. Doesn't mean I have to forgive him right away. The scarecrow has been there since before you were born. Before *I* was born. Before anybody here was born." Frank pointed down the street. "Two blocks down, take a left. You'll be at the medical center. The morgue is next to it, so you're going in the right direction even if things don't work out for your dad. You can entertain yourselves. Goodbye."

Frank turned and walked back the way they'd came.

"I didn't mean to offend him," Oliver insisted.

"He overreacted," said Trisha. "It's a gigantic scarecrow

in the middle of the village. Of course it's creepy. This whole place is creepy. Let's go find Dad."

As they hurried down the road, Trisha couldn't shake the feeling they were being watched. She glanced over her shoulder. Had the scarecrow moved? It stood there, its smile stitched on its face, but now it felt like a smirk.

CHAPTER THREE

Since they no longer had to follow Frank, the twins ran down the street. They passed businesses instead of homes—a pharmacy, a small grocery, a barbershop—but there didn't seem to be people around. It felt like a ghost town.

Then a man stepped out of a sandwich shop and gave them a friendly wave. They waved back. Better not to anger anybody else by being rude.

The twins turned left and saw two men wheeling a gurney down the street. Belinda walked beside them. Dad was on the gurney, covered with a gray blanket, except for his head, which was on a pillow. There were no sidewalks, and he bumped down the cobblestone street, but Oliver hoped the pillow was protecting him.

Belinda had warned them about being a distraction. However, when she noticed Oliver and Trisha, she smiled and waved them over.

Dad's eyes were still closed, but they'd already put on a new bandage.

"Your father is going to be fine," Belinda said. "Lucky for him and lucky for you, there's a shortcut to the dock. We're going to run some tests and keep him overnight for observation. Don't worry—we'll make sure you're kept safe during the night. I'm pleased to say that neither of you are going to be orphans anytime soon."

Oliver was baffled at how she delivered this good news— did real doctors actually talk like that? He was relieved that they weren't going to be orphans, but what a strange way to say it. The people in this village seemed to have very odd social skills.

But still, Dad was going to be okay!

As long as they could trust these people.

He wasn't entirely sure that they could.

"We're going to take him inside," said Belinda. "The mayor has been made aware of the situation, and he'll discuss the details with you two."

"Out of curiosity," said Trisha, "how far are we from the nearest city?"

Belinda's face hardened. "Are you saying that you'd rather transfer your father to a big-city hospital?"

"I'm saying that we have no idea what's around here. We were surprised to find this village. We want to make the best decisions for him. Or call our mom so she can."

"The mayor will go over all the information with you. You'll like him. He's very good with children. Now, if you'll excuse me..."

She held the door open, and the men wheeled Dad inside the building. From the outside, it looked like any of the other buildings on the street, though it did say ESCROW MEDICAL CENTER above the door. There were no windows, which seemed more than a little odd. Without looking back at the twins, Belinda followed the men into the building.

"I don't like this," said Oliver.

Trisha nodded. "Me neither."

"Does this look like a hospital to you?"

"I don't know what a hospital would look like in a small village like this. But I'm not sure what else we can do. We're twelve. Our phones don't work. We're not gonna wheel Dad into the woods to find someplace better."

"What now?" asked Oliver. "Wait for the mayor?"

"I guess. I don't want to go too far."

They stood there for a moment. Trisha looked like she was going to cry, and Oliver tried to decide if he should give her a hug or not.

"Dad looked okay, though, right?" he asked. "He didn't look any worse than when we left him. They seemed like they knew what they were doing. There's no reason to think they can't help him."

"They acted really weird," said Trisha.

"Yeah, they did. Really, really weird. But they aren't used to new people. It doesn't mean they aren't good doctors." Oliver wasn't sure he believed this, but it felt good to say it, and maybe it would make Trisha feel a little better too.

A man stepped out of a doorway a few buildings away. He was short, had a sunburnt bald head, and wore a white suit. "Hello!" he called out to the twins.

Oliver and Trisha exchanged a glance, then waved.

"Hello!" the man called out again. Did he mean for them to join him?

The man made his way over to them and gave a big friendly grin. "You must be our special guests. My name is

Jarvis Clancy. I'm the mayor of Escrow Village. And your name, young lady?"

"Trisha."

Mayor Clancy stuck out his hand. "That's a great name! The best name I've heard lately. Pleased to meet you, Ms. Trisha!"

"Thank you," said Trisha, warily shaking his hand.

Mayor Clancy turned his attention to Oliver. "And you, young man?"

"Oliver."

"Oliver! Another great name! I like that almost as much as your sister's name! Your parents named you well. Shake my hand, Mr. Oliver. Don't be shy."

Oliver shook his hand, trying not to recoil at the mayor's clammy grip.

"Now, I know you youngsters are concerned, but I assure you, your daddy is getting the best care. The scarecrow will make sure he comes through this experience better than ever, I can promise you that. And while the circumstances of your visit aren't the most pleasant, I'm going to make sure you enjoy your time in our village as much as possible."

Oliver *really* wanted to ask what the mayor meant about the scarecrow, but he decided it wasn't the time.

"Thank you," said Trisha. "Is there a phone we could use? We need to call our mom and let her know what's happening."

"Oh, goodness, no. I'm so sorry," said Mayor Clancy. "We're a long way from any cell phone towers. That sort of thing doesn't interest us."

"I meant a landline. The doctor had one."

"We all have telephones, but only to call other people in the village. We have no need to call anybody else."

"Not even for emergencies?"

"We handle our own emergencies."

"Not for supplies or anything?"

"You ask a lot of questions," said Mayor Clancy with a chuckle. "That's okay. I remember being young and inquisitive. How old are you? Eight? Nine?"

"Our twelfth birthday was yesterday," Oliver told him.

"Oh, well, look at me not knowing how to guess people's ages. Happy birthday. As a gift, I'd like to invite you to Agatha's Café. Tell her you're a close personal friend of mine, and she'll give you a free meal. I'm talking about lunch *and* dessert. You're not too old for dessert, are you?"

Oliver's stomach growled. It had been a while since breakfast. "That's very kind of you," he said. "Thank you."

"My pleasure. She already knows you're coming. The café is down the street, past the scarecrow. Do say hello as you go by. When we have news, we'll find you."

"Thanks," said Trisha.

"May the scarecrow watch over you." Mayor Clancy reached up as if to politely tip his hat at them, but since he wasn't wearing a hat, he touched his forehead. Then he walked away.

"Do you think he was lying?" asked Trisha. "Surely they have some way of contacting the outside world. We have to tell Mom what's happening. We're supposed to check in every day."

"I know," said Oliver. "She's going to be really worried."

"How do we know they're even trying to help Dad? How do we know they aren't...I don't know, using him for spare parts?"

Oliver's stomach dropped. "Are you serious?"

"No. But I don't like this."

"Neither do I. No matter how weird this place is, it's still probably our best option to help Dad."

"Then what next?" Trisha asked.

"Maybe...we get a free meal? Talk to people in the café? The sign said the population is nine hundred and ninety-nine. At least one of them has to be normal."

"I *am* kind of hungry."

They walked toward the center of the village, back toward the scarecrow. As they got closer, a chill ran through Oliver's body. He shuddered. An old woman sat on one of the benches, looking up at the scarecrow with a serene smile on her face. She didn't acknowledge the twins as they passed.

Oliver regretted offending Frank, but that scarecrow was seriously creepy.

Soon they reached Agatha's Café. A sign on the glass door read OPEN TO FRIENDS.

A bell above the door tinkled as they went inside. A few other customers were seated at tables, and a woman in a dirty apron greeted them, her red hair piled high on her head.

"You must be Oliver and Trisha! Welcome! I'm Agatha. The mayor said to take good care of you. Please, have a seat." She led them to a booth near the back and handed them a couple of menus. "Can I start you with something to drink? Water? Milk? Grapefruit juice?"

"Water is fine," said Trisha.

"One water," said Agatha, writing it down on her pad. "And for you?"

"Do you have Coke?"

"How about iced tea instead?" She wrote in her pad again. "Now you two look over those menus and decide what you want to eat. I'll be right back to take care of you."

Agatha left. Oliver glanced down at the menu. He expected it to be filled with bizarre selections like velociraptor meat or poison ivy salads, but it was normal café fare like sandwiches and hamburgers.

The other people in the café were doing a very poor job of pretending not to stare at them. He tried to focus on the menu.

A moment later, Agatha returned with their drinks. She set them on the table and grinned. "Do you need a few more minutes? It's on the house, so don't be shy."

"I'll take a hamburger and fries," said Oliver.

"That's a good choice," said Agatha, noting his order on her pad. "How many fries?"

"Excuse me?"

"How many fries would you like with your hamburger?"

"Oh, uh, I'm not sure."

"Twenty? Twenty-one?"

"Twenty sounds good."

Agatha wrote that down, then looked at Trisha. "And you?"

"I'd also like a burger with twenty fries."

"Well, you two sure are making my job easy today, aren't you? I'd like to offer my condolences—no, *condolences* isn't the right word—I'd like to offer my *sympathy* for your father. I'm told he'll be perfectly fine, but still, it must be scary for you."

"It is," said Oliver. "Thank you."

"But you'll get him back on his feet and then be on your way, right?"

"Yeah. Belinda said they might need to keep him overnight for tests, but yes, we're hoping to leave as soon as we can."

Agatha froze. "You're spending the night?"

"Is something wrong?" Trisha asked.

Agatha's smile had vanished. "No, why do you ask?"

"You look concerned, like something's wrong."

"Oh, no, no, no. I just wasn't expecting you to stay after dark." She lowered her pad slowly and then gave them a great big smile. "I'll be right back with the very best hamburger and fries you've had in your life." Her smile faltered for a moment, and then she quickly left.

CHAPTER FOUR

Trisha and Oliver sat silently while they waited for their food. It was an uncomfortable silence, but Trisha couldn't think of anything to say except that she was worried about Dad, and she didn't want to talk about that. Especially not with everyone staring at them.

At least their food came out quickly.

"Here you go, sweetie," said Agatha, placing a huge burger in front of each twin. She winked. "Eat up, and let me know if you need anything else!"

After she left, Oliver smiled. "Should we count the fries?"

Trisha didn't respond.

"I was joking," Oliver clarified. "You know, because it's strange to order a specific number of fries."

"I know. It just wasn't funny," Trisha told him. She usually loved his jokes, even if she often pretended that she didn't. "I mean, it was funny, but I'm not in the mood to laugh."

"It wasn't one of my better ones."

"It was fine." Trisha lifted the top bun off the burger. There was lettuce, onions, a pickle, and a tomato. It looked like a perfectly normal hamburger. In fact, it smelled delicious. Trisha didn't want to be paranoid that her lunch might be poisoned or drugged, but everybody in Escrow was behaving very oddly, and she didn't want to gobble down a potentially tainted burger.

"What's wrong?" Oliver asked.

"Nothing."

Her brother picked up a fry and popped it into his mouth. He winced and quickly breathed in and out with his mouth open, trying to cool down the fry.

Trisha smiled. Here she was, wondering if their food was safe for consumption, yet Oliver didn't pause long enough to make sure it wouldn't burn his mouth. Typical.

Finally, he chewed and swallowed. "Too hot," he said.

"I noticed."

"But good." He poured some ketchup onto his plate and dunked a second fry before eating it. Then he picked up the burger with both hands and took a bite. "Oh, man, this is amazing," he said, his mouth full.

"Best burger you've had in your life?"

"Pretty close." He chewed in total bliss.

Trisha continued to stare at her plate. She had to eat. She couldn't help Dad if she was weak from hunger. Why would Agatha tamper with their lunch? Trisha imagined eating their burgers...then waking up strapped to an operating table or in a dark coffin, having been buried alive. Was she being ridiculous?

Just to be safe, she picked up the butter knife and cut her hamburger in half. It looked fine. Not that she knew what a drugged burger would look like—it wasn't as if there'd be whole pills sticking out of the meat.

She took a bite. It *was* a really good burger. And she was ravenous. The chances of this being a dangerous hamburger were so low that it wasn't worth starving to death.

One of the other diners, a woman who was too old to be their sister but not old enough to be their mom, walked over to their table. She twisted a lock of her long red hair around her index finger. "Hello."

Trisha, who unlike her brother did not talk with her mouth full of food, finished chewing and swallowed. "Hi."

The woman let out a nervous giggle. "Are you from the outside?"

"Yeah, I guess. I mean, we don't live here, if that's what you're asking."

"What's it like?"

Trisha shrugged. "It's about the same." She didn't really want to get into this kind of discussion.

The woman looked deeply disappointed. "Oh."

"We don't have a giant scarecrow in the middle of the city," offered Oliver.

"You don't?" The woman seemed genuinely surprised.

"Nope."

"Then what protects you?"

"Emergency workers, first responders—we just call nine-one-one."

"Oh." The woman nodded, though it was clear that she didn't understand.

"Mildred." The man she'd been sitting with gestured to her. "Leave the children alone so they can eat."

"But they're from *the outside*."

"I know that. Everybody knows that. But you're bothering them."

Mildred bit her lip as if she might burst into tears. "I'm not bothering you, am I?"

"No," said Trisha, lying. Mildred was making her really uncomfortable.

Mildred looked back at the man. "See? They like talking to me." She returned her attention to Trisha. "Is there a sun where you come from?"

"Of course we have the sun," said Oliver.

Trisha glared at her brother. Sometimes she thought they were five years apart instead of him being thirteen minutes older. "We do," Trisha told Mildred politely. "Had you heard differently?"

The man got up from his table and took Mildred gently by the arm. "It's time to leave them alone," he said. "We don't want their fries to get cold."

"But I enjoy talking to them, and they enjoy talking to me."

"She's not bugging us," said Trisha.

The man squeezed Mildred's arm, not so gently this time. "I'm not going to tell you again." He led her back to their table.

Trisha glanced around the café. The other diners looked away.

"Let's eat and get out of here," Trisha told Oliver.

He nodded and popped two fries into his mouth at once.

As soon as they finished gobbling down their meal, Agatha appeared, holding an enormous hot fudge sundae in each hand. "Dessert time!" she gleefully announced, smiling so broadly that her gums showed. She set a bowl in front of each of them.

There were three oversize scoops of vanilla ice cream, an absurd amount of hot fudge, whipped cream, nuts, and five or six cherries. Trisha couldn't have eaten the whole thing if she tried. "Thank you," she told Agatha. "You didn't have to do that."

"You're guests in our village, and you need something to take your minds off your dad's awful condition. Eat up!"

Trisha decided not to worry about the sundae being poisoned. She took a bite, and it was easily the best ice cream she'd ever had. She wanted to get out of Escrow as soon as possible, but she had to admit the village had great food.

She ate a few more bites until she was too full to

continue. Even Oliver, known affectionately by Mom as the Bottomless Pit, was full before he'd devoured half the sundae.

Agatha returned to their table. "How is it?"

"Amazing, thank you," said Trisha.

Agatha smiled. "I'm glad you're enjoying it. Finish up before it melts."

"Oh, no, I'm stuffed. But it was the best hot fudge sundae I've ever had."

Agatha's smile disappeared. "It's the best hot fudge sundae you've had in your entire life, but you're already done with it?"

"Well, I mean, I just ate a gigantic burger."

Agatha's voice became low and quiet, the way Mom's did when they got in trouble and she used their full names. "The mayor asked me to take care of you two. I made you this special dessert, gave you extra cherries, and you can't be bothered to finish it?"

"I'm sorry," said Trisha. "If I'd known you were making dessert, we would've shared one. This thing is huge."

"It was supposed to make you happy." Agatha pursed her lips. "I guess where you live there are hot fudge sundaes everywhere you look. Here in Escrow, we make our own ice cream, and we make supply runs to the outside world as rarely as possible. People here finish their meals. I know that's not your problem, but the ice cream you're letting melt could've been given to somebody else."

Trisha picked up her spoon. This wasn't worth fighting over. "I didn't realize that," she said. She took another bite of ice cream, as did Oliver. Agatha stood there for a moment, eyeing them suspiciously as if she thought they might sneakily slide the ice cream onto the floor, then went to take care of one of the other tables.

"I can't believe how weird this place is," Oliver whispered.

Trisha ate a few more spoonfuls of the sundae, but she was starting to feel queasy. There was no way she'd be able to finish without throwing up. And if she threw up, that would be more of an insult. She pushed her bowl away.

It was hard to imagine being forced to eat dessert. When they were younger, they had to clean their plates of nasty vegetables like eggplant and asparagus. But Trisha had never been pressured to eat ice cream. This should have been the ultimate fantasy, not a nightmare!

Agatha returned to the table. She looked at their bowls with disapproval. "Seriously?"

Yes, they were kids, and it was a free meal, but the owner of a café didn't have the right to make them eat something they hadn't even ordered.

"I'm sorry," Trisha said. "The ice cream is delicious, but it's too much."

Agatha's eyes flashed with anger. Genuine anger. She picked up the half-empty bowl, and for a moment, Trisha thought she was going to smash it into her face, like a clown with a cream pie.

"This is why we don't like people from the outside," Agatha said. "They're ungrateful and rude. You try to be nice, but they simply don't appreciate it."

Trisha had no idea what to do. She wanted to stand up for herself, but she didn't know how much longer they'd have to stay in this village, and she didn't want to make enemies.

"We weren't ungrateful," she said slowly and evenly. "This was all very kind of you."

"Actions speak louder than words, young lady. That's a lesson most children learn by your age. If your father were alive..." She paused. "If your father were *here*, I'd give him a good talking-to about how he raised you two."

Oliver pushed back his chair and stood. "We're going now."

"Nobody's stopping you," said Agatha. But she took a step to the left, putting herself between Oliver and the door.

The other customers in the café stood too.

A trickle of cold sweat ran down Trisha's back. Were these people going to stop them from leaving? They weren't skipping out on their bill. There was no bill. Why shouldn't they leave? This was unthinkable. And yet...

"Let's go," Oliver told her.

Trisha nodded. Her legs started to buckle as she got up, and she had to grab the chair to keep from losing her balance.

Nobody else moved.

Agatha held the bowl tightly as if she might shatter it in her grip. Her face was contorted with ugly rage. Over two kids not finishing a hot fudge sundae!

Oliver walked around the table to Trisha. Together the twins slowly walked toward the door. The café owner and customers watched.

Don't run. Don't run, Trisha told herself. She and Oliver pushed open the door, and the bell chimed, although this time it sounded less cheerful.

"Hey," said Agatha.

Trisha reluctantly turned back from the sidewalk. "What?"

"The scarecrow sees you."

"The scarecrow sees you," the customers echoed as the door swung shut behind them.

CHAPTER FIVE

"We have to get out of here," said Trisha. The twins picked up their pace, as if Agatha and the others might chase after them like zombies. "We can't trust any of these people."

"I agree," said Oliver. And he *did* agree, completely, but there was still the problem that Dad was seriously injured.

Or dead?

No. He wasn't dead. Agatha had misspoken and corrected herself.

Oliver hated being trapped in a place that made him feel so unsettled. But they couldn't wheel Dad out on a gurney, take him back down to the canoe, and resume floating down the river, hoping to find help someplace else.

Or could they? If they couldn't trust anybody in the village, should they get Dad out, even if he still needed medical attention? What kind of awful things might happen to the three of them if they stayed here? What if they were prisoners forever? Sure, that idea seemed ridiculous, but these people had a gigantic scarecrow in the middle of their village! Who knew *what* they were capable of doing?

"Let's go back to the medical center," he said. "Demand to talk to Dad."

"What if he's still unconscious?"

"They can't keep us away from our own father. We have a right to see him. We won't leave until they let us."

Trisha nodded. "Let's do it."

They walked in that direction. With each step, Oliver felt sick from the ice cream. He could only imagine how his sister felt. He got the impression Agatha would've had them eat those sundaes until their stomachs exploded. Literally. And then she'd stitch their bellies back up and make them eat some more.

When they reached the medical center, Oliver pulled on the door handle. Locked. Why would a medical center be locked? What if somebody needed help?

There was no doorbell, so Oliver knocked.

Nobody answered.

"Hello!" he called out. He continued knocking. If somebody didn't answer soon, he'd start kicking the door and screaming.

Finally, the door swung open. Mayor Clancy stood there, looking angry. Why was the mayor there? He was a politician, not a doctor.

"What?" he asked.

"We want to see our dad," said Trisha.

"I already told you that isn't possible."

"We still want to see him."

"I'm sorry, I don't take orders from children," said Mayor Clancy. "I understand that you were very rude to Agatha too."

"She called you?" asked Trisha.

Mayor Clancy nodded. "She was very upset. I'm not sure how children behave where you come from, but around here, we expect them to be polite and grateful."

Oliver didn't want to get into an argument about an over-size hot fudge sundae. "We're here to see our dad," he repeated. "We're not leaving until we do."

"Is that so? You're not leaving until you bring your filthy germs into a sterilized environment? Are you *trying* to kill your father?"

"Then let us get scrubbed in," said Trisha. She'd seen

some of those doctor dramas Mom liked to watch on TV. "We'll take showers, wash our hands up to our elbows. We'll put on whatever masks we need."

"No. This is a place for treatment. There's no room for little kids to be running around."

"We're not four-year-olds," said Trisha. "We just want to see our dad. And like my brother said, we're not leaving until we do."

Mayor Clancy smiled. "That almost sounds like you're threatening me. I'm *terribly* curious. What exactly do you plan to do if I refuse?"

"We'll call the police," said Oliver.

The mayor threw back his head and barked out a laugh. "The police? On me? In my own village? What exactly do you think is going to happen, young man? The sheriff is going to pin me against the floor while a pair of dirty children wander the halls?" He laughed again. "I have a stressful job without much in the way of levity, so I thank you for that. But now I'd like you to leave."

"We're not leaving," said Oliver.

"Then perhaps you'd like to spend the rest of the day in one of our jail cells. I assure you, you won't get hamburgers and ice cream in there."

Trisha couldn't believe she was doing this, but she couldn't back down, even if they were kids and he was the mayor. "Maybe you didn't hear my brother," said Trisha. "We have to see our dad."

Mayor Clancy stepped outside, closing the door behind him. "You two have been quite the disruption. What you need is to find some inner peace. Therefore, I'm going to make you a deal." He pointed to the village square. "I want you to go over there and sit on one of the benches. Do one hour of silent reflection. No talking. No fidgeting. Simply bask in the protection of the scarecrow. If you do that for a full hour, I'll believe you're calm enough to see your father. How does that sound?"

It sounded stupid to Oliver. If anything, that creepy scarecrow would make Oliver feel less calm. He didn't want to look at that thing for an entire minute, let alone an hour.

And what if it was an hour they couldn't afford to lose? If the medical center wasn't taking good care of Dad, they needed to get him to a real hospital as soon as possible. They couldn't waste time with this silent reflection nonsense.

Oliver and Trisha glanced at each other, unsure of what to say.

"This offer won't last forever," said Mayor Clancy.

Oliver clenched his fists in frustration. They shouldn't *have* to stare at a scarecrow for an hour to get to see their father. But what else were they supposed to do? They had no power. Unless he was prepared to shove the mayor out of the way and rush inside—and Oliver had to admit he was considering it—they had no choice.

"That isn't necessary," said Trisha. She took a deep breath for the mayor's benefit. "We're calm."

"You don't look very calm to me. Spending some time with the scarecrow will do you good. You haven't made the best impression on the folks in this village, and I think you should take this opportunity to repair the damage."

"Do you promise we'll get to see him?" Oliver asked.

Major Clancy held up his hand. "As mayor of Escrow Village, I give you my word."

Oliver glanced at Trisha. She nodded. "Okay," Oliver said. "You have a deal."

"Excellent, excellent," said the mayor. "You two walk on over and have yourselves a seat. Look at the scarecrow and let your mind wander. I'll check on you in an hour."

He opened the door to the medical center, stepped inside, and closed it behind him without another word.

"I'm not sure I believe him," said Trisha.

"Me neither."

"Maybe he needs an hour to hide Dad's body. Bury it somewhere."

Oliver hadn't considered that. He suddenly wanted to cry.

"I could knock again," he said. "When he answers the door, we push right past him. He can't stop both of us."

"He'll put us in jail."

"We came here to get Dad help, but now he needs to be rescued."

Trisha was quiet for a really long time.

"For now, we have to trust the mayor," she finally said. "But only for now. If he goes back on his promise, we'll... I'm not sure what we'll do, but we'll get in there somehow."

"So I guess we have to stare at that stupid scarecrow?"

"I guess so."

The twins walked over to the village square. The same elderly woman sat on a bench in the front row, her eyes closed, a peaceful smile on her face. Oliver and Trisha sat in the back row so as not to disturb her.

The scarecrow, its arms outstretched, still seemed to peer at them through its button eyes.

Oliver hated looking at it. It was terrifying. Though he supposed that was the whole point of a scarecrow.

It loomed motionless above them. Oliver watched carefully for the signs of breathing that he knew were only in his imagination.

The scarecrow looked like it might lean down and eat him in one bite.

Or a few bites. That would be worse.

Oliver tried to reassure himself. He and Trisha were together. And there was nothing to be afraid of. It wasn't a monster before them. The scarecrow was made of very large blue overalls filled with straw. Its head was burlap. Its eyes were buttons. (Where did they get buttons that big?) Its mouth was stitched on. It was big and scary looking, but it was completely harmless.

He still hated looking at it.

If the old woman could close her eyes, so could he.

Oliver shut his eyes and tried to think about something fun. Video games. They'd get Dad out of here, go home, and he could play all the video games he wanted. After everything they'd been through, Mom wouldn't set a time limit.

Closing his eyes wasn't helping. It made the situation worse. Who knew what the scarecrow was doing while he wasn't looking? Maybe it was leaning forward, its stitched mouth opening to reveal fangs...

He opened his eyes. The scarecrow's mouth hadn't changed.

But was the scarecrow closer?

No. It hadn't moved. It was exactly where it had been a few seconds ago, which was exactly where they'd first seen it.

Besides, if it *had* moved, Trisha would have noticed.

There was a gentle breeze. It felt good in the heat, but it also made the scarecrow wobble a bit.

That wasn't the breeze, Oliver, he imagined the scarecrow saying.

At least he hoped he was imagining it.

I'm watching you, Oliver. When you blink, I blink too. I'm hungry, Oliver. You didn't finish your dessert, but I sure will. Oh, you'll be a tasty, tasty dessert.

"Stop it," he said.

"Stop what?" Trisha asked quietly, gesturing not to disturb the old woman.

"Nothing." Oliver couldn't believe he'd said that out loud. He couldn't let this scarecrow mess with his head. It was a giant roughly made stuffed doll. Absolutely nothing to be frightened of. If he wanted, he could walk up there and fling its stuffing all over the village square. It was harmless.

Totally harmless. Only a little kid would be scared of it.

Okay, that wasn't true. The scarecrow was as tall as a house. Lots of people might be intimidated by its size. If a person came home and found that thing in their backyard, they'd scream in terror. *But* he also had to recognize that it was not actually alive, not speaking to him in his mind. It was a stationary object and could not hurt him in any way.

Are you sure about that, Oliver?

Very sure.

If I came after you, are you sure you could get away? I have longer legs. If I chased you down the streets of the village, I think you would be an easy catch. Where would you hide, Oliver? Where would you hide?

Shut up. Oliver was very careful not to say this out loud. He was getting chills—actual chills—from this, like he'd suddenly gotten a fever.

Don't be rude.

I said to shut up, Oliver repeated.

Maybe I'll eat your sister first. You can listen to her scream. Oh, she'll be so scared, and there'll nothing you can do to save her. Nothing at all.

"Oliver?"

Oliver flinched at the sound of Trisha's voice.

"Are you okay?"

"Yeah, why?"

"You were whimpering."

"I was not," he insisted. Oliver hoped Trisha didn't notice how badly he was sweating.

He wasn't going to make it a full hour.

Of course you won't. I'll devour you and your sister long before the hour is over.

The scarecrow's head tilted a bit.

He had *not* imagined that!

"Did you see that?" he whispered.

"What?"

"Its head moved!"

"Yeah, it was the wind."

"Are you—?" Of course it was the wind. When a gust blew through town, a scarecrow filled with only straw would move.

But how did he know it was only filled with straw?

He could see straw protruding from various places, but how did he know that was *all* that was in there?

The scarecrow could be filled with anything.

It could be filled with guts.

It could be filled with the bones of its victims.

If Oliver tore off the burlap sack that was its head, a misshapen face could be underneath.

Or just darkness.

Oliver bit the inside of his cheek. He was definitely not going to make it the full hour.

CHAPTER SIX

Trisha was worried about Oliver. He had whimpered, and he was drenched in sweat. He looked absolutely terrified.

Though she was admittedly a little braver than her brother, it had been a long time since either of them were frightened of ghosts, the boogeyman, monsters under the bed, or anything like that. This was a scarecrow—yes, an enormous one, but still only a scarecrow—so she wasn't sure why he was reacting like this.

But with everything else that had happened, she was stressed out too.

Oliver was trembling so much that if this hadn't been a stone bench, it would be quivering.

Trisha wasn't sure what to do. Oliver didn't like being consoled by his sister. Still, she placed her hand on his.

He seemed to relax.

Trisha looked up at the scarecrow. She imagined it singing "If I Only Had a Brain" from *The Wizard of Oz*. Maybe this village also had a giant tin man and cowardly lion.

It really did seem like the scarecrow was looking back at her, even though it had button eyes. Just a trick of the sunlight. When she moved her head back and forth, the sunlight's reflection in its eyes moved as well. That's all it was.

This was going to be one boring hour.

What if Dad is more seriously injured than we thought?

Don't think about that, Trisha told herself. She'd never been much of a worrier, although, to be fair, she'd never been in this kind of situation.

What if Dad was dead? It would explain why the mayor wouldn't let them see him.

Why wouldn't the adults tell them the truth? Why hide it?

Maybe the mayor thought they needed the scarecrow's peace to cope with the bad news.

Trisha sighed. She missed Dad. She missed Mom. If this was what it was like to be an adult—having to make important decisions but not really being in charge of how they worked out—she was way less eager to be a grown-up.

Okay, Trisha couldn't think about all the ways things had gone wrong or could continue to go wrong. For all she knew, it was indeed a germ issue keeping them from seeing their dad. They'd spend the next hour staring at the scarecrow and hope for the best afterward. She'd had plenty of practice sitting around being bored—Oliver had terrible taste when he got to choose the film on movie night.

Oliver was still all sweaty, though he didn't seem to be trembling anymore.

She stared at the scarecrow for a while, trying not to fidget and mostly succeeding.

Fine. She'd admit it. It was kind of creepy.

She had no idea why this thing would give anybody inner peace.

The scarecrow's arms swayed a bit in the breeze.

She heard somebody walking behind them and tried to see who it was.

Tried to.

She couldn't turn her body to look away from the scarecrow.

It was as if her neck were frozen. She tried again, but she

couldn't move her head at all. She couldn't even glance over at Oliver.

She attempted to say something to him. She couldn't speak.

Trisha couldn't move a muscle. Her entire body was paralyzed.

Her heart raced. She was starting to freak out.

A voice whispered in her mind, *Why would you want to turn away? Don't you like the way I look?*

This wasn't happening. She'd fallen asleep. Once she and Mom had watched a documentary about something called sleep paralysis. That must be what was happening to her. This was a dream.

Oh, Trisha, you're not having a dream. This is no nightmare. You were asked to look at me for an hour, and I'm going to make sure you follow the rules.

She tried to scream for help, but no sound emerged.

Stop fighting me, Trisha. Just relaaaaaax. Focus on your breathing. Slow, deep breaths.

Trisha tried to scream again.

You're making me unhappy, Trisha. Stop resisting. Slow, deep breaths, like a good girl. Because if I want to, I can make you stop breathing altogether...

Did Oliver know what was happening to her? She couldn't turn to look at him. Was it happening to him as well?

You'll beg me to let you take just...one...breath... You'll feel like you're drowning, but you'll be sitting right there. All because you didn't follow the rules.

"Isn't it wonderful?"

Suddenly, the spell was broken. Trisha spun around to see who was behind her.

"Oh, I'm sorry," said a man in a fancy blue suit. "Didn't mean to startle you." He gestured to the scarecrow. "But isn't it wonderful?"

Trisha took a deep breath to steady herself—and make sure her lungs were working properly. "Ah, yes," Trisha said hesitantly. "It's wonderful."

Oliver quietly harrumphed beside her.

"Don't let its size intimidate you. It protects us. It would never harm us."

"I feel very protected." Trisha hoped she didn't sound sarcastic.

"It's older than the village."

"Seriously?" she asked.

"Yes. The scarecrow was not brought to the village. The village was built around the scarecrow. Nobody who lives here can remember a time when the scarecrow wasn't here, and we have some very old residents." The man grinned. "Anyway, I apologize if I disrupted your concentration. We almost never see new faces around here, so it's a pleasure to have you young folks becoming one with the scarecrow. I'll leave you to it." He nodded at her, then at Oliver, then walked away whistling.

"I hate this scarecrow," Trisha whispered to Oliver.

"Me too." Oliver frowned. "Did something happen to you before the man started talking to us?"

"Did something happen to *you*?"

"I asked you first," Oliver said.

The old woman on the front bench turned and glared at them. "There's an awful lot of talking back there."

"We're sorry," said Trisha.

"Don't apologize. Stop talking." The woman turned back toward the scarecrow.

Trisha scooted right next to her brother, then whispered into his ear, "What happened?"

Oliver whispered back, "I said I asked you first."

"I couldn't move, and I thought I heard it talking in my head."

Oliver's mouth dropped open, and his face went pale.

"Did you hear it too?" Trisha asked.

Oliver started to shake his head, but then reluctantly nodded.

"What did it sound like?"

"Low," Oliver whispered. "Raspy. Maybe *raspy* isn't the right word. You know Uncle John, who we met at that family reunion? He'd chain-smoked cigarettes all his life, and it messed up his voice. That's kind of what the scarecrow sounded like."

Trisha felt queasier than she had after gorging herself at lunch. That's how the voice had sounded to her too.

She didn't believe giant scarecrows could communicate through thoughts, but she also wasn't going to waste time trying to come up with a logical explanation. For now, she was simply going to accept what was happening and worry about the science—and the implications—of it later.

She didn't need to tell Oliver the voice she heard sounded the same. He could see her expression. He knew.

"What do we do?" he asked.

The old woman turned around again. "I've asked you to be quiet. Clearly, it won't help to ask you again." She stood. "Now you've ruined it for me."

"I'm sorry," Trisha told her. She was usually considered

to be extremely well-behaved by adults; this was a new experience.

"Yes, well, sorry and a jar of pickles will get you a jar of pickles." The woman walked away.

"I've never heard that one before," said Oliver.

"We'll joke about it later." Trisha wiped her forehead. She was sweating too. "Let's play along. Sit here and pretend we're feeling all peaceful. But don't look at it."

Oliver nodded. "We'll look down like we're deep in thought."

The twins sat on that hard wooden bench, side by side, staring at the cobblestone.

They could get through this. All they had to do was avoid looking at the scarecrow. And since Trisha didn't *want* to look at the scarecrow, it would be really easy. Then, after the hour was done, they'd make the mayor honor his promise.

Sweat trickled down Trisha's face and dripped from her chin onto the stone.

Inside Trisha's head, somebody chuckled.

Do you really think that's all it takes, Trisha? Not looking at me? Do you think it's that simple?

"Do you hear that?" she asked, unable to hide the fear from her voice.

"Hear what?"

I'm not talking to your brother. I'm talking to you. You're the smarter one, aren't you, Trisha? You're stronger, braver... You're the leader. He'll do whatever you tell him to, won't he?

"Leave me alone."

What if you told him to do something horrible? He'd do it, I bet.

"No."

I think he would. What should we tell your brother to do, Trisha? Does he like heights? Maybe he should practice his balance on one of the roof peaks.

"I said to leave me alone!" Trisha was fighting back tears.

I don't like you, Trisha.

"I said—"

"She said to leave her alone!" Oliver told the scarecrow. Then he frowned. "No," he said. "No, I won't do it."

Trisha put her hand on her brother's arm. "What's it saying?"

Oliver shook his head. "No. You can't make me. I won't do it. I won't. I won't. I won't."

Trisha stood. She accidentally caught a glimpse of the scarecrow in the process, but nothing about it had changed. She grabbed Oliver by the shoulder and pulled him to his feet.

He was crying. He sniffled and wiped his eyes on the back of his hand, then looked away from her, embarrassed.

"It's okay." Trisha tried to reassure him.

"It's not okay. It told me to grab your hair and pull as hard as I could. See how much I could tear out."

Trisha stared at her brother in horror. Then, to break the dark mood, she forced herself to smile. "Well, I'm glad you didn't. Thanks."

Oliver shrugged. "It was the least I could do."

"We can't stay here. Let's go."

The twins walked away from the scarecrow, trying to appear casual. Trisha kept waiting for it to bid her farewell, but the scarecrow remained silent.

"That wasn't anywhere close to an hour," said Oliver.

"I know." Trisha glanced around. The street was empty. That didn't mean they weren't being spied on, but as far as she could tell, they were alone. "I think I have a plan. We need to keep as calm as possible. Think happy thoughts. Do everything we can to stop being scared and keep the scarecrow out of our minds. Literally."

"None of my thoughts are happy right now."

"Then fake it. We're going back to the medical center, and I need you to follow my lead. Don't argue with anything anybody says. Smile. Relax."

"Ha," Oliver said, then nodded. "I'll try."

"We'll walk slowly. Pull ourselves together."

They very casually strolled along the street. Trisha's heart was racing, and she had to keep wiping sweat off her forehead, but she felt better the farther they got from the scarecrow. By the time they reached the medical center, she felt...well, she still felt awful, but she could pretend.

They both stood in front of the building, taking deep breaths.

Then Trisha knocked on the door.

They waited.

She didn't want to knock again too soon, so she counted to sixty in her head before knocking again.

The door opened. It was Mayor Clancy again. Didn't this medical center have a receptionist?

"What do you want?" he demanded.

Trisha blinked with confusion. "What do you mean? We had a deal."

The mayor looked at his watch. "It hasn't even been fifteen minutes."

Trisha turned to Oliver, feigning surprise. "That can't be right, can it?" She looked back at the mayor and smiled. "I guess we went deeper in our mediation than I realized. I could've sworn it was an hour."

"I thought so too," said Oliver. "I was so relaxed, I almost felt like I was asleep."

The mayor raised an eyebrow.

"We can come back," said Trisha. "I'm sorry. Time didn't seem to have any meaning while we were with the scarecrow."

"No, it's fine," said the mayor, not sounding at all like it was fine. "Come on in. I'll take you to your daddy."

CHAPTER SEVEN

The twins followed Mayor Clancy inside. As soon as they walked through the door, they were in a narrow hallway with a linoleum floor and white walls. There was no receptionist or waiting area, and it was lit by too-bright fluorescent lights that made a humming sound.

Oliver felt like they were walking into a dangerous situation. But after demanding to see Dad, they couldn't shrug and bow out. *Sorry, changed our mind—this place seems kind of unnerving.*

"Close the door behind you," said the mayor over his shoulder.

Oliver reluctantly did as he was told.

They headed down the hall, then turned a corner and walked down another hallway.

Then another corner. Another hallway.

They didn't pass a single doorway. Where were the doors? Where were the rooms?

They turned yet another corner. And then another. And another.

The hallways were getting shorter each time. Were they in a maze?

No, not a maze. A spiral. A square spiral.

There was something incredibly wrong here. No hospital would have this kind of layout. It made absolutely no sense.

Trisha walked with a perfectly content expression on her face, even though she had to be thinking the same thing he was. They followed the mayor as if this were completely normal.

Finally, the mayor stopped and turned to face them.

"Your father hasn't woken up from his coma yet," he said. "What you're going to see may upset you, which is why you needed the serenity that the scarecrow brings us. Your young minds might not have been able to cope otherwise. I can't let you into the room—germs—but you can peek through the glass."

"Thank you," said Trisha in her special polite voice she used with grown-ups.

"Yes, thank you," Oliver echoed.

They followed the mayor around the final corner. The hallway dead-ended at a steel door with a small window.

Oliver and Trisha squeezed past him and looked inside.

Dad was lying on a bed in a small room. His eyes were closed. He was *covered* in wires of all colors—red, green, blue, yellow, white... There were hundreds of wires. Maybe a thousand. There were so many of them that it was hard to say for sure.

Oliver gasped.

He could tell Trisha was disturbed by the sight, but she did a good job of hiding it aside from the death grip she had on his hand.

Oliver looked at Dad's bare arms. The wires led to several pieces of equipment that were arranged on each side of the bed. It didn't look like normal hospital equipment. They were metal boxes of various sizes, and aside from the wires, there wasn't much to their appearance except for the occasional knob and blinking light.

Oliver didn't know what to do. That huge scarecrow

was creepy, but this was flat-out disturbing. "What happened to him?"

"We're trying to save your daddy's life," said the mayor. "We almost lost him a couple of times. I know it looks messy in there, but we're keeping him alive."

"He hurt his head," said Oliver. Dad's head was indeed wrapped in thick bandages. "Why does he need the rest of that?"

"Oh, he hurt far more than his head," said the mayor. "I promise you. He wouldn't be alive if you hadn't found us."

It was very possible that Dad got scraped up when the current pulled him along the river floor. And Oliver, who was not a medical professional by any stretch of the imagination, wouldn't have known if Dad had internal injuries. But these wires? They didn't make any sense. Yes, almost all of Oliver's medical knowledge came from movies and TV shows, but this was clearly *wrong*.

"What are the wires for?" asked Oliver.

Mayor Clancy smiled. "Have you ever been in a hospital?"

"Yes." Oliver had broken his arm when he was nine. And they'd visited their Aunt Jenny a few times, a memory he didn't like to think about.

"And did it look anything like this?"

"No, sir."

The mayor proudly pointed at the window. "This isn't the kind of care your daddy would be getting in a big-city hospital. But you know what? He'd likely be dead if you hadn't stopped at our dock. I don't mean to be harsh, but there's no other way to say it. Your daddy was hurt far worse than you realized, and because of what we did for him, he's alive."

"Where are the doctors? The nurses?" Oliver asked. "The doctor who brought him here. Where is she?"

"Belinda has done her work and is getting some much-needed rest. Don't you worry—if your daddy's condition changes, she'll get an alert and be here right away."

"Why are you here?" asked Oliver, hoping it wasn't one question too many.

Mayor Clancy seemed genuinely surprised. "Why shouldn't I be?"

"You're the mayor. Don't you have other stuff to do?"

The mayor gave Oliver a pat on the shoulder. "You make a good point, young man. Most mayors wouldn't spend their day keeping tabs on an out-of-town patient. But I run a village of just under a thousand residents, and they're all law-abiding citizens. I can't remember the last time the law put anybody in jail. It may have been to give people shelter before a storm came through. Not trying to downplay my influence, but Escrow more or less runs itself. So, when something unusual happens, like a family from the outside world showing up, well, I take a personal interest."

Oliver nodded. He still thought it was strange that there wasn't an actual medical professional watching over Dad.

"You look concerned," said Mayor Clancy. "Before I was the mayor, I was a doctor. I know my way around setting a broken bone. You don't need to worry. Besides, if I sustained a horrific injury, there's nowhere I'd rather be than within spitting distance of the scarecrow."

Oliver looked back through the window. "Do you think he'll wake up soon?"

"I think he will. And he'll be proud of you. Both of you. But now he needs rest."

Oliver didn't want to abandon Dad while he was attached to all those wires and tubes like some mad scientist's experiment. For all he knew, they were draining Dad's blood.

"You're right," Trisha told the mayor. "It's time for us to go. Thank you for taking such good care of him."

"No problem at all, young lady."

They followed Mayor Clancy back through the spiraling hallway until they reached the exit. The mayor turned the lock and opened the door. "I'd like you to spend more time on those benches. The scarecrow will ease your anxiety. I'll come get you later, and we can figure out where you're going to spend the night."

Oliver *so* did not want to spend the night in this village. He knew there was no way out of it, but he couldn't imagine spending one more second here. He just wanted to take Dad and go home!

"Thank you again," said Trisha. "I'm still worried about my dad. I'm really scared." Trisha's whole body began to quiver.

"It's all right, young lady. It's natural."

Then Trisha began to cry. She threw her arms around the mayor and sobbed into his chest. As she cried—heaving, racking sobs—the mayor awkwardly patted her on the back and assured her that everything was going to be all right. He looked uncomfortable. He obviously wasn't used to this sort of emotion.

Trisha wasn't one to cry, so her tears got Oliver choked up as well. He took a big calming breath, like before he was going into a new level of a video game. They could do this. They had each other, even if Trisha was hugging a weird stranger.

His sister's wailing lasted for at least two minutes. Finally, she sniffled and wiped her nose on the back of her hand. "I'm sorry," she told the mayor. "I got snot all over your jacket."

The mayor grimaced at the mention of snot but said, "It's washable. Now you two run back to the scarecrow. It'll do you good."

"We will."

The mayor went back inside. Oliver heard the lock turn.

"It'll be okay," Oliver told Trisha. "They say Dad is getting the care he needs. I'm sure Dad will be fine." He wasn't certain he believed that, but his sister definitely needed consoling.

"That's not why I was crying. I mean, seeing Dad like that made it *easy* to cry, but that's not why I did it."

Oliver gave her a confused look.

She held up a ring of keys and smiled. "I stole these."

CHAPTER EIGHT

Oliver gaped at her. "You..."

"Stole his keys," said Trisha. "If I needed a hug to feel better, it certainly wouldn't be from that guy."

There were nine or ten keys on the ring, and none of them were labeled. Trisha tried to slide one into the lock. It didn't fit.

Oliver seemed stunned that his twin sister was such a skilled thief. "Don't you think he'll notice?"

"He might. But if we take the one we need and leave the rest of the keys by the door, he might think he dropped them." The second key didn't fit either, nor did the third, but the fourth one did. She took it off the ring and put it into her pocket. Then she dropped the key ring.

"Okay. What now?" Trisha looked toward the village square. "I don't want to go near that thing again."

"I totally agree," said Oliver. "Let's walk around and figure out our plan. We'll stay close enough that the mayor doesn't freak out if he looks for us, but far enough away that the scarecrow can't affect us."

"How far do you think that is?" Trisha asked.

"I have no idea."

They walked halfway to the village square. The annoyed old lady was gone, but a man and woman about Mom and Dad's age sat on one of the benches, hand in hand, looking up at the scarecrow.

"Let me know if you hear it talk to you," Trisha whispered.

Oliver nodded. "Oh, I will. Don't worry."

They gave the benches a wide berth and settled themselves on a low wall by what looked like a community garden. Trisha could still see the medical center from here, so if the mayor came out, they could say they were stretching their legs.

It was silent, almost peaceful there, given the circumstances. Unlike when they were camping, there wasn't the usual background buzzing of bugs or reliable rumbling of the river. There weren't sounds of lawn mowers or kids playing like back home either. Every so often a breeze blew, rustling the tree leaves, but she couldn't even hear birds chirping.

"The scarecrow's efficient, that's for sure," Trisha said. Suddenly, the quiet felt too quiet.

"Uh-oh," said Oliver. "It's Frank."

He was right. So much for some quiet to develop their plan. Though maybe he could help them rescue Dad.

Frank walked over to them, a proud look on his face. "I told you it wasn't creepy." Frank looked at Oliver. "Did you apologize?"

"Apologize? You mean, to the scarecrow?"

"Yes. Who else would you apologize to? Abraham Lincoln?"

"He did." Trisha spoke up, hoping to avoid an argument. "I heard him. I'm not sure if it forgave him, but he said he was sorry for calling it creepy."

"Of course he forgave him," said Frank. "The scarecrow doesn't hold grudges."

"That's good to know," said Oliver.

"I don't hold grudges either. You're new in town, and I was wrong to expect you to understand right away." He motioned for the twins to follow him to the benches. "Let's sit together. Maybe we can become great friends."

"That sounds really nice," said Trisha. "But we've been sitting on those stone benches for a long time. Our legs fell asleep. We were walking around to get the blood circulating again." She slid from her perch and stretched her legs a little, like before her team practices, hoping that would be convincing. Clearly, Frank wouldn't be their answer to getting out of Escrow.

"Oh," said Frank, sounding so disappointed that it was almost heartbreaking. "I thought it might bring us closer together, is all."

Trisha had no immediate response, but it didn't matter. Frank kept talking.

"I looked over here a few minutes ago. You weren't here. I'm not calling you a liar. It's not nice to call people liars. All I'm saying is that I walked by the scarecrow about four or five minutes ago, and neither of you were there. I've been watching since then, and neither of you sat down on the bench."

Trisha was silent for a moment. "Right," she said.

Violence was never the answer, but if this were a movie, and if they'd been indoors and she had a frying pan, this would've been the point when she bonked him on the head to knock him unconscious and dragged him into a closet until they figured out what to do.

"But like I said, I'm not calling you a liar."

Oliver chimed in. "We sat with the scarecrow for a while, and it, uh, was the best experience of our lives. And we didn't want...we didn't want you to... It's nothing personal, but we didn't want..."

"You didn't want me to spoil it?" asked Frank.

"Not *exactly* that."

"I understand." Frank turned and slowly walked away.

"I feel terrible," Oliver whispered. "But I didn't know what else to do. Maybe we'll find a way to make it up to him."

"Maybe," said Trisha. She was stealing. They both were lying. This village really wasn't bringing out their most admirable qualities.

Trisha almost expected the scarecrow to make some sort of comment. Maybe she'd imagined it talking to her, even though the same thing had happened to Oliver.

"What do you think we should do?" Oliver asked.

"I think Dad's in danger. I don't believe the mayor when he says they're trying to help him. I don't believe anything he says."

"Dad looks more like an experiment than a patient," Oliver agreed.

"Right. So we need to get him out of there."

"You mean...*take* him?"

"Yes."

Oliver scratched his forehead. "You really think the mayor and Belinda would leave him completely alone? That's the plan we should start with?"

"I took the key, didn't I?" Trisha asked, "Do you have another idea?"

Oliver hesitated. "Let's get back in the canoe and go down the river until we find a place with a working phone. Call the police. Have *them* get Dad out of there. I don't like leaving him behind, but we're not doing anything for him now anyway, and it's a lot less risky than trying to kidnap Dad. I mean, how are we supposed to get him down to the canoe without anyone noticing, down the river, and maybe through more rapids?"

Trisha considered that for a moment. "That's actually a way better idea. Maybe the scarecrow stole some of my brain cells."

"We should go," said Oliver. "Don't tell anybody. Leave before someone tries to stop us."

"Yeah. I'm in."

But Trisha, said a low, raspy voice in her head, *we were getting along so well. You don't really want to leave me, do you?*

Trisha didn't respond, out loud or in her mind. She walked with Oliver toward the dock.

You're making me angry, Trisha.

She noticed its voice was quieter than before. She picked up her pace, and Oliver followed.

So angry. You're making a terrible mistake, Trisha. A deadly mistake.

Trisha continued to ignore it.

But she couldn't ignore Frank, who was headed toward them.

"Where are you going?" he asked.

"Taking a walk," said Oliver.

"Where to?"

"Around. We haven't seen much of the village, so we figured we might as well explore."

"First you didn't want me to spoil your time with the scarecrow, and now you're exploring the village? I could show you around."

"What's going on?" asked an unwelcome and familiar voice. Trisha let out a sigh of frustration as the mayor approached. She wondered if somebody had called the medical center. For all she knew, the buildings were filled with people spying on the outsiders.

"You can't trust them," Frank said.

"Oh, I know that." Mayor Clancy said. "Where were you two going?"

Trisha decided there was no reason to lie. "We're leaving."

"I beg your pardon?"

"We appreciate everything you've done for our dad, but we can't stay. We need to get Dad home. So we're going to head down the river until our phones work or we find somebody who can get help."

"Oh, no, no, no, no, no," said the mayor. "That would be preposterous. We're not going to let a couple of twelve-year-olds leave the village this late in the day. What if you got hurt?"

"We'll be fine," said Trisha.

The mayor shook his head. "Not a chance. You could go missing and never be seen again."

"You can't stop us."

"Of course I can. Your mother isn't here, your father is incapacitated, and you're both minors. If I let you go down to the river and something bad happened, it would be all my fault. I'm sorry to lay down the law, but you're spending the night in Escrow, whether you like it or not."

"We won't let you kidnap us," said Trisha.

"Don't be so melodramatic. Nobody is being kidnapped. We're simply keeping you safe." Mayor Clancy sighed. "You seem to think I'm a tyrant, and nothing could be further from the truth. Believe me, I'll be happy when you two troublemakers are on your way. But you're in my village, and I'm responsible for everyone here. Tomorrow morning, at first light, I'll send somebody with you downriver."

"We want to go now," said Oliver.

"It's not up for discussion. You'll be staying with Edith tonight, and you will follow all her rules—I mean *all* of them. If I find out you're disobeying her in any way, I'll throw you in jail." Mayor Clancy pointed at Oliver and then at Trisha. "That is not an empty threat. You two can sit in a cell until your daddy is recovered enough to take you home. And if he doesn't recover..." The mayor shrugged.

"You should throw them in jail now," said Frank.

"Calm down, Frank. We all make mistakes." Mayor Clancy turned toward the twins. "I've made a very generous offer. Do you agree?"

Trisha did not agree, but she said, "Yes, sir."

The mayor flashed a cruel grin. "Excellent. Let's go meet Edith."

CHAPTER NINE

Edith was probably not a witch. Probably.

She was the most witch-looking person Oliver had ever seen. If he were trying to be funny, he'd guess that she was about a hundred and fifty years old. If he were trying to be serious, he'd guess ninety. Maybe ninety-five. Though if he found out she was indeed a hundred years old or more, it wouldn't surprise him.

She had long stringy gray hair. Warts. And her voice sounded like a witch's, minus the cackle.

She hobbled across the wooden floor of her small home toward the fireplace, upon which a black pot rested. She lifted the lid, stirred the contents with a wooden spoon, and took a long, deep whiff. "Ahhhh," she said, smiling and exposing her one tooth. "The porridge is ready."

Oliver didn't know porridge was an actual thing. He thought it only existed in "Goldilocks and the Three Bears."

He and Trisha had offered to help her cook, but Edith had waved them off, insisting that they were her guests. Her fingernails were so long that they had to make accomplishing daily tasks quite a challenge.

After she scooped out their servings, Edith sat on a wooden chair with her bowl in her lap. Oliver and Trisha sat on the floor, which was covered with dust but was at least not covered with bugs, dead or living.

The porridge was the nastiest substance Oliver had ever eaten. And that included some of the meals they'd made toward the end of camping trips with Dad. It was similar to what he imagined eating wet cement would be like. He was glad Edith wasn't a conversationalist, because the porridge stuck to his tongue. But he and Trisha were gracious, making the necessary "mmm" and "yum" sounds as they choked it down. Oliver was prepared to accept a second helping if it were offered, but to his intense relief, Edith didn't offer.

"Good, wasn't it?" asked Edith, rubbing her belly.

"Delicious," said Trisha.

"Scrumptious," said Oliver.

Edith took their bowls and dropped them into the sink. She hobbled over to the room's single window and peered outside. "Ah, the sun has set. Darkness is coming. Are you children scared of the dark?"

"Not since I was really little," said Oliver.

"Perhaps you were smarter when you were younger," said Edith. She pulled the curtain closed. "I have three rules for guests in my home. First rule: Do not make noise. I don't sleep well, and the sound of footsteps or whispering will keep me awake."

"We'll be quiet," Trisha promised.

"Second rule: Do not steal from me. I'll know. I keep track of all my possessions."

"We'd never steal from you," Oliver assured her. "You've been very nice letting us stay with you tonight."

"Third rule, and this is the most important one by far: Do not venture outside in the night. It's not safe for you. It's not safe for anybody. If you leave this house, it will be the last anybody ever sees of you. Trust me on that."

"Is it because of the scarecrow?" asked Trisha.

Edith nodded. "The scarecrow doesn't like people being outside after dark. It makes it harder for him to protect us. And if we don't care about his protection, we might as well..." She paused. "You're too young to hear about such things. Just don't go outside, no matter what you hear."

"All right," said Oliver. "Those rules make a lot of sense."

"I go to bed when darkness falls, and so will you. I'll show you to your bedroom."

Oliver wasn't tired, but they clearly weren't going to play games, tell stories, or talk by the fire like they did while they were camping. He supposed he was lucky they weren't spending the night on the stone benches by the scarecrow.

Edith opened a door for them, a door that creaked so loudly that even somebody making a horror movie would say, *Hey, let's tone that down a bit.* There was no bed, but there were some blankets on the floor. It didn't look *too* uncomfortable, no different from their sleeping bags on the ground.

Oliver and Trisha went into the room. Edith began to close the door behind them. "That's not necessary," Trisha said. "We'd rather sleep with the door open."

"That won't do at all," said Edith. "Your breathing will keep me awake."

She closed the door before Oliver could protest. It felt like they were in a dungeon. There were no windows or lights in the room, so they were cast into total darkness.

"What do we do?" asked Oliver, whispering as softly as he could.

"We'll wait for Edith to go to sleep. Then we leave as quietly as possible," said Trisha. "If we have to open this door half an inch at a time, that's what we'll do."

Oliver nodded, then remembered Trisha couldn't see him in the utter darkness. "Okay."

They sat on the floor in the dark, not speaking. Oliver wanted to check his phone to see how much time had passed, but they'd both turned off their phones to save battery power.

What was Mom thinking now? Was she sick to her stomach with worry, or had she convinced herself that they simply couldn't get cell phone reception? Even if she contacted the authorities, she wouldn't be able to give them much in the way of useful information. Maybe if another day passed, they'd search the river and find their canoe at the dock, but they weren't going to send a full search party this soon, right?

Oliver wasn't sure how long they should wait. How long did it take an old woman to fall asleep?

They didn't have to guess. Before long Edith began to snore. Loudly. So loudly that it was as if she were right there in the room with them.

Very slowly, Oliver twisted the knob and started to push against the door.

It creaked as noisily as before. Oliver froze.

Edith's snoring stopped.

He stood there, unmoving for what felt like an eternity, waiting for Edith to bellow, *I told you not to break the rules! Now you must pay the price!* But after a moment, her snoring resumed.

Oliver wished they had some oil to grease the hinges.

He opened it a smidge more. Another creak.

This time her snoring continued.

A bit more.

And more...

Her snoring stopped again.

Oliver heard her roll over. He silently counted to one hundred, but the snoring didn't resume. Had she fallen back asleep? Maybe the creak of her mattress was her getting out of bed. Maybe she was waiting to ambush them with the fire poker. Maybe she *wanted* them to break her rules, so she could punish them...

Trisha nudged his arm. They had to stick to the plan. Worst-case scenario, they could outrun a ninety-five-year-old woman. Unless she placed a curse upon them.

Oliver pushed the door open a little more. If they turned to the side and held their breath, they could squeeze through the opening. He carefully tiptoed through, and Trisha followed.

He wished he could close the door behind them so Edith wouldn't notice they were gone if she got up in the middle of the night, but that was too dangerous with those squeaky hinges. They tiptoed to her front door, moving as carefully and quietly as possible. The only illumination was moonlight through the window, which would have to be enough. Oliver was kind of a klutz, but he made it to the front door without tripping over furniture or doing any wacky slapstick antics.

Hopefully, the old lady's front door wouldn't creak as much.

Oliver turned the knob and gently pulled. Piece of cake. They snuck out of the house and very gently shut the door behind them.

Except for the moonlight, it was completely dark outside. Not a single streetlamp illuminated the road, and no lights were visible in any of the houses. It didn't appear that any of Escrow's 999 residents stayed up past dark, let alone ventured out of their homes after nightfall.

Oliver could've used the light on his phone, but he didn't want to risk attracting attention. They'd simply have to walk slowly and carefully along the cobblestone street. Fortunately, the village was laid out in nice straight rows, so they wouldn't get lost, and it had only taken about ten minutes to walk from the village square to Edith's home.

A few steps later, Trisha stumbled. He grabbed her arm to hold her steady, and they resumed walking.

"Are you scared?" he asked.

"Yes," she said. "Terrified. You?"

"Almost wetting my pants."

It was easier to think that, hey, maybe Mayor Clancy was being totally honest with them. That tomorrow morning they'd have an expert guide with a speedboat to get them to the nearest town after sunrise. And then a helicopter would pick up Dad, and everything would be perfect, and they'd never have to think about Escrow again.

But no. There was something deeply sinister about this whole place, and they had to get Dad out of here before it was too late. If it wasn't already too late.

They continued walking. It was scary how silent it was. Did nobody stay up after the sun went down? Read a book by flashlight or at least by candlelight?

As their eyes adjusted and they got more comfortable walking in the dark, they picked up their pace. The streets were well maintained, and Oliver hadn't noticed any potholes or loose rocks in the daylight. A relatively quick walk seemed safe enough. They didn't know what was happening with Dad, and they didn't know if Edith's warnings were justified. They had to treat this as if every single minute counted because, for all they knew, every single minute did!

Up ahead, they could see the village square, and the...

Wait, that couldn't be right. He squinted.

"Do you see it?" he asked.

"See what?" asked Trisha.

Oliver didn't answer. He didn't want his sister to think he'd lost his mind. Besides, they were still too far away to know for sure without more light.

As they drew closer, he could tell it wasn't his imagination or a trick of the darkness.

Trisha spoke before him. "The scarecrow's gone!"

CHAPTER TEN

The scarecrow couldn't just get up and walk away... could it?

Trisha's eyes had adjusted to the night well enough that she could see there was no scarecrow in the village square. It's not like it could hide in the darkness. This scarecrow was the size of a two-story house! And it simply wasn't there.

Trisha tried not to panic. There had to be a logical explanation.

If the people of Escrow were so enamored of their scarecrow, it was possible they took it down every night to bring it indoors, out of the elements, and put it back up in the morning. It could be in a storage area somewhere. There was no reason to freak out over the missing giant scarecrow.

Oliver sounded like he was on the verge of hyperventilating.

"Calm down," she said, then shared her theory.

"Okay, yeah, okay," said Oliver. "That makes sense. There's no reason to have it standing here if everybody's asleep. Makes total sense." His breathing hadn't slowed.

"Forget the scarecrow," said Trisha, as if such a thing were possible. "We have to focus. Let's go get Dad."

They joined hands and ran toward the medical center.

If they weren't so distracted by the missing scarecrow, they would've remembered that running on a cobblestone street in the dark was a very bad idea, which was proven when Oliver tripped and fell.

He let out a yelp as he landed.

"Are you okay?" Trisha asked as she crouched next to him.

"Yeah, I'm—" Oliver let out another yelp.

"What did you hurt?"

"Nothing. I'm fine."

Trisha pulled Oliver to his feet. He winced in pain.

"I can walk. Let's go," insisted Oliver.

Oliver limped, but it didn't slow them down. The medical center wasn't very far, but they had a lot of walking to do after this, and Trisha desperately hoped Oliver could keep up.

He stopped.

"What's wrong?" Trisha asked.

Oliver stared into the distance, his eyes wide with horror.

Trisha looked in that same direction. What was her brother seeing?

Wait...

Visible above one of the houses, something was moving. Something enormous.

"Is that—?" Oliver asked, the words coming out as a frightened gasp.

Trisha was almost positive that, yes, that was the scarecrow's head peeking above a roof as it walked behind one of the homes. "Keep going. We're almost there. Hurry." As difficult as it was, Trisha didn't look back.

They reached the front door of the medical center. Oliver was still trembling and looking over his shoulder.

Trisha reached into her pocket. It took her a moment to fish out the key, and then she tried to slide it into the lock.

It wouldn't fit.

Why wouldn't it fit? She'd tested it! Had the mayor changed the locks? Had they come out here for nothing?

"It's walking around!" Oliver said, way too loud. "The scarecrow is walking around!"

Trisha had to focus. Oliver wasn't the only one trembling—her hands were quivering. She took a deep breath, tried to keep as still as possible, and slid the key into the lock. It turned.

Inside, they were hit with a blast of light so intense that it felt like it was going to melt their eyeballs. Trisha and Oliver squeezed their eyes shut, then very slowly opened them to adjust their vision as they stepped into the building. Trisha yanked on the door handle, but she caught herself and closed it gently so it wouldn't slam it shut.

"How's your foot, really?"

"It hurts. I can walk on it, though."

"Good."

They headed down the bright corridor. Each time they turned a corner, Trisha expected somebody—or some-*thing*, claws and fangs bared—to leap out at them, but nothing did.

Trisha carefully peeked through the window into their father's room.

Dad was lying there, still connected to various machines, still unconscious.

A woman was in the room as well, her back to them. Trisha was pretty sure it was Belinda.

For all they knew, Edith had discovered that her houseguests were missing and called the mayor, who was on his way with reinforcements. They couldn't wait for the perfect moment. They had to act now.

Trisha sat on the floor, then knocked on the door.

She and Oliver got into position and waited.

Waited.

Waited.

They scooted back as the door opened.

Then they kicked the door as hard as they possibly could, slamming it into Belinda. Oliver cried out in pain as Belinda cried out in surprise. They heard her fall to the floor. Trisha wished there'd been time to come up with a clever way to outwit their opponent, but sometimes you just had to kick a door.

Trisha grabbed the edge of the door, threw it all the way open, then tackled the doctor. She didn't want to get *too* violent—they weren't going to drop one of the metal boxes on her head or anything like that—but they needed to subdue her, quickly.

Trisha hated to do it, but she punched Belinda in the gut, really, really hard.

The doctor let out a loud grunt, clutched her stomach, and curled into the fetal position.

"I'm sorry! I'm sorry!" Trisha blurted. Aside from her one week in Tae Kwon Do, she'd never hit anybody. She played contact-free sports!

She started to tell Oliver to find something to tie Belinda up with, but Oliver was already on it. He picked up a coil of red wires, and while Trisha held the struggling doctor down, Oliver tied her hands behind her back. Though the wires didn't bend easily, he finally got it done.

"What is *wrong* with you little brats?" Belinda cried out.

"We're here to get our dad," Trisha told her, even though that was probably very obvious.

"Are you kids out of your mind?"

Yes, most likely they were, but Trisha didn't answer the question. "We don't want to hurt you."

"You punched me!"

"I know. I'm sorry. I won't do it again if I don't have to."

Belinda tried to pull her hands apart. The wires weren't designed to bind people's hands together, and Oliver's work wasn't going to last very long.

"I need you to quit doing that," Trisha said.

Belinda didn't stop.

"I *really* need you to quit doing that. I don't want to use Tae Kwon Do, but if I have to, I will." Trisha left out the fact she'd only learned a few moves during a unit in gym class.

Belinda stopped moving. "Do you kids even have a plan?"

"You don't need to worry about that," Trisha said. Belinda might be trying to keep her talking and distracted until help arrived, so they needed to get Dad out of here right away.

Trisha and Oliver walked over to the bed. Dad looked awful. His chest was rising and falling under the blanket, but his face had no color. He didn't look peaceful. For someone who was in a coma, he looked...afraid.

Oliver pulled the blanket down to Dad's waist and gasped. Dad was *filled* with wires. Every half-inch square of his body seemed to have a wire sticking into it.

Trisha wanted to cry again. "What did you do to him?"

"Kept him alive."

"No! He didn't need this!"

"Are you a doctor now?" asked Belinda. "Have you graduated from medical school since you brought him here? That's quite an impressive accomplishment."

Trisha had to focus. She had no idea how much time they had. Oliver reached for one of the many, many wires.

"May I give you a warning?" Belinda asked, sitting up. "If you pull out those wires, you're going to kill your father. Let me say that again: *if you pull out those wires, your dad will die.* Was I clear?"

"You're lying."

Belinda sighed with frustration. "No. Have you heard the phrase *death by a thousand cuts*?"

"I think so."

"If you pull out one of those wires, there'll be a little blood. No big deal. If you pull out two of them, a little more blood. Again, no big deal. Sort of like slapping a mosquito on your arm after it's full. But if you keep pulling out the wires, he's going to bleed more and more, and I promise you, he won't even make it out of this building, much less to wherever you're planning to take him."

"Don't listen to her," Trisha told Oliver.

"Sure, don't listen to the doctor keeping your father alive," said Belinda. "Go ahead. Pull out a wire. I wouldn't pull out one in his neck, but one in his arm should be okay."

Oliver pinched one of the wires in Dad's upper right

arm between his index finger and thumb. He gently pulled on it. It wouldn't come loose. He tugged harder.

"You're going to have to pull harder than that," said Belinda. "They're in there pretty good."

Oliver yanked harder. On the third try, the wire popped free, followed by a thin trickle of blood.

"She's right," Oliver said, looking panicked. "He'll bleed to death if we try to pull all these out."

"What if we cut them?" Trisha asked.

"Did you bring wire cutters?" asked Belinda.

"You must have some in here. Where are they?" Oliver hurried over to a cabinet and started opening the drawers.

"You're wasting your time," said Belinda. "I'm happy to let you figure it out for yourselves, but really, you're wasting your time."

Oliver took a large knife out of the top drawer. He returned to Dad and pressed the blade against one of the wires. The wire wouldn't cut, so he switched to a sawing motion.

"I told you, those things are sturdy," said Belinda. "Think about how long it would take to cut through them all. All night, I'd guess. But I haven't even gotten to the part where you're wasting your time. Wait for it...wait for it..."

Oliver continued to vigorously saw away. Finally, the knife broke through, and a bit of blood squirted out of the wire.

"There we go!" said Belinda. "Those wires are hollow. It's more accurate to call them tubes, really. So not only will it take you all night to cut through all of them, but you'll have the same problem you will if you try to pull them all out. If you don't mind a dead dad, go right ahead and keep doing what you're doing, but my recommendation is that you accept defeat."

Oliver's shoulders slumped.

Trisha didn't want to give up. She couldn't. There had to be another way.

"I'm pretty unhappy about this," said Belinda. "Yet I also understand your point of view. You just want your father back. I can't honestly say I'd do the same thing in your shoes—I'd plan things out a little better. But I don't see any reason to make you suffer for your mistake, so I'll make you a deal. Don't tell anybody that you got the upper hand on me, and I won't tell anybody you were here. We start everything from scratch. No winners, no losers."

Trisha wasn't sure how to respond to that.

"Mayor Clancy is a reasonable man," said Belinda. "But

if he finds out you broke in and attacked me, it won't matter that you're not even teenagers yet. I know what it's like on the outside. They'd say, oh, they're just kids, we'll go easy on them. That's not how things work here. I *promise* you don't want the mayor to know what you did."

"You're saying you'll just let us leave?"

"After your brother unties me. It goes both ways. You say nothing, and I say nothing."

Trisha hated this, but she couldn't see how they had any choice. "Go ahead," she told Oliver, who knelt beside Belinda and started untying the wires. He'd only been working on them for a few seconds when Belinda yanked her hands free.

"Who did they make you stay with?" Belinda asked.

"A lady named Edith."

"Ah, yes. The oldest lady in town. I guess the mayor wasn't trying to make you comfortable. If you're smart, and I sincerely hope you are, you'll head right back there as fast as you can."

"What about the scarecrow?" Oliver asked.

"You noticed it was gone, huh?"

"We saw it moving."

"Good. Then I don't have to dance around the truth. You

need to get back to Edith's house. Don't bother trying to get shelter with anybody else—they won't open the door for you. Quickly, before the scarecrow catches you."

"What will it do to us?" Oliver asked.

"I don't know. Do you know why I don't know? Because people in this village are smart enough to stay inside their locked homes after dark. I wish you could stay here, but obviously you can't, so you need to get back to Edith's house before you solve the little mystery of what happens if the scarecrow catches you. Go *now*."

Trish took one last look at Dad, then reluctantly turned and hurried down the hallway, Oliver quickly limping behind her.

CHAPTER ELEVEN

Oliver and Trisha left the medical center. Now that they were out of the painfully bright fluorescent lights, the darkness felt heavy again.

Where was the scarecrow?

Though they couldn't see anything, they knew which direction they needed to go, and the twins speed walked down the street. Oliver's foot definitely didn't feel very good, but it wasn't as if he could sit down and put an ice pack on it. He forced himself to keep pace with his sister.

He really wished his eyes would hurry up and adjust to the dark. The scarecrow could be anywhere.

Very soon, they were going to have to figure out what to

do about Dad, but for now, they just needed to get to safety. Maybe it would turn out that Mayor Clancy *hadn't* been lying, and tomorrow morning they'd be back on the river, on their way to get help.

"Is that it?" Trisha asked, pointing to the left.

"Where?"

"Over there!"

"I don't see it!"

Trisha stumbled but didn't fall. "Maybe I was wrong. Yeah, I was wrong. It's hard to see anything." It was dark enough anyway, but right now a cloud was covering the moon.

"We'll see it coming, though," said Oliver. "There aren't many places for a giant scarecrow to hide."

They kept moving. But they'd only gone a few more steps before Oliver thought he saw it, off in the distance, about as far away as the length of the football field at school: a shadow darker than the night surrounding them walking behind one of the houses.

Was it too much to ask for this village to have just one light?

Whatever it was stopped moving. Maybe it was his imagination.

Oliver stared at it as he walked, trying desperately to see what might or might not be lurking behind that house.

He suddenly was almost positive that there *was* something there. And that it was looking at them.

No, that was ridiculous. He wouldn't be able to tell if the scarecrow looked at them from that far away. He wouldn't be able to tell if it saw them in broad daylight, not with its button eyes. His imagination was messing with him.

But...whether it was looking at them or not, that *had* to be the scarecrow over there.

It began to move again.

Though Oliver didn't scream—they were still on a stealth mission after all—he really wanted to when the scarecrow walked between two houses, heading straight for them.

There was still another row of homes separating them from the monster, yet Oliver didn't feel the least bit safe.

Hello, Oliver.

"It's talking to me!" Oliver tried his best to keep his voice steady, but he couldn't.

Why are you outside, Oliver? Don't you know what happens to those who venture outdoors after dark? Didn't anybody warn you?

Trisha grabbed his hand. "Let's go!"

Oliver wanted to tell his sister to save herself, leave him behind, and run as fast as she could back to Edith's house. But he also didn't actually *want* her to run away and leave him behind, so he didn't say anything.

In the movies, enormous creatures like Godzilla and King Kong moved slowly. They lumbered along on their path of destruction. The scarecrow, meanwhile, was fast.

It was catching up to them!

I'm coming for you.

Then the scarecrow stepped into the street in front of them.

Almost as if the scarecrow controlled the clouds—though, of course, that was ridiculous—the moon came fully into view. And in the moonlight, Oliver could clearly see its face. It tilted its head as it regarded them, and then the scarecrow's stitched-on smile curled up at the edges.

It took a great big step toward them, making the most of its long skinny legs.

The twins turned and fled, back the way they'd come.

Oliver couldn't help but look back. The scarecrow took another huge step, closing the distance between them.

"Yes, we can!" Trisha shouted. Oliver wondered what the scarecrow had said to her in its raspy voice. Probably something sinister, like, *You can't outrun me, Trisha.*

If that was what it had said, the scarecrow was right—they couldn't outrun it.

But that didn't mean they couldn't escape.

The twins dashed through somebody's front yard.

The scarecrow took another step, its foot landing so close to Oliver that the movement ruffled his hair. He was certain it could have stomped on him if it wanted.

Oliver and Trisha kept moving, staying as close to the houses as possible. It was better than being out in the open. Maybe they could find a place to hide.

They circled a house, returning to the front yard. All the yards were almost barren. No trees. No sheds. No doghouses. No cars, and in fact, no driveways.

They pressed themselves tightly against the house and remained completely still. The scarecrow might not be able to see in the dark any better than they could. Maybe if they were motionless, it wouldn't know where to find them.

Oliver listened carefully.

Nothing.

All he could hear was Trisha's frightened breathing. He couldn't imagine that the scarecrow would give up this easily.

Then there came a footstep. It didn't rattle the ground, but it was unmistakably the step of the scarecrow.

The twins didn't move, didn't breathe.

I know where you are.

The scarecrow leaned around the side of the house, its head so close that Oliver could have reached out to touch it.

They ran.

Pain shot through Oliver's foot with every step, but he wasn't about to slow down.

The scarecrow chased them.

Oliver was so scared and confused that he wasn't sure if they were running toward Edith's house or away from it.

One step hurt so bad that it felt like Oliver's foot had burst underneath him.

"I can't!" he said, out of breath. "My foot..."

The scarecrow was still in pursuit. Step. Step.

Oliver and Trisha both screamed.

The scarecrow bent over, leaning its head down toward them.

Oliver had been terrified enough when it was only a scarecrow with a burlap sack for a head, button eyes, and a stitched-on smile. But now its button eyes glowed red. And the burlap split apart as its mouth opened wide, revealing enormous sharp teeth, like those of a great white shark.

That horrible mouth came right at him.

Oliver moved out of the way just before it tried to bite him in half.

You smell delicious, Oliver.

They ran.

The scarecrow's foot slammed down beside them. Once again, Oliver was confident it could have crushed them flat if it wanted.

They screamed again.

Why were no lights turning on in any of the houses? Why wasn't anyone opening their door to investigate the noise? What was wrong with the people in Escrow?

The scarecrow grabbed for Trisha and missed.

"We have to see if somebody will let us in!" Oliver said, hoping Belinda's warning was wrong.

They ran to the nearest house. Both of them began to pound on the door.

"Help us!" Trisha shouted. "We're being chased!"

The scarecrow leaned toward them again. Its eyes still glowed.

They pounded on the door as hard as they could. The people inside wouldn't let them get eaten, would they?

The scarecrow's wide-open mouth came right at

Oliver. He could feel the hot stink of its breath on his body.

With his good foot, Oliver kicked the scarecrow in the face.

The scarecrow leaned back and frowned, as if surprised its prey had fought back.

Oliver noticed that one of its teeth was now stuck in his shoe.

Maybe it would go away. Maybe the scarecrow recognized they wouldn't simply sit back and be devoured. Maybe the monster would slink back to the village square, defeated.

The scarecrow did not run.

It stared at them, and then it smiled. It licked its stitched lips with its burlap tongue. Once again, it opened its mouth wide.

There was no place to escape.

At least not if Oliver and Trisha wanted to be respectful of other people's property. And at this particular moment, they didn't. People who refused to answer their door to kids about to be eaten by a giant scarecrow deserved to have their windows broken.

They kicked together at the front window. It took a few tries, but finally the glass shattered. They scrambled through, careful of the sharp edges, as the scarecrow slammed its mouth shut, trying to bite a chunk of Oliver.

The twins rushed to the other side of the room, hoping the scarecrow couldn't reach in, grab them, and drag them back outside.

They were safe. For now.

A light turned on—an actual interior light!—and a man in white pajamas emerged from a bedroom.

"No!" the man shouted. "No, no, no! You can't be here!"

Trisha pointed to the broken window. "The scarecrow is trying to get us!"

"Don't you think I know that?"

A woman stepped out behind him. Another door opened, and a boy who looked a few years older than the twins poked his head out.

"We can't help you," the man said. He raised his voice to a shout, as if calling out to the scarecrow. "We're not helping them! They broke in without our permission!"

"Please," said Oliver. "Let us stay here until it goes away."

The man shook his head. "Get out of here!"

"Get them out, Harold!" the woman wailed. "Get them out now!"

"Make them leave, Dad!" the boy pleaded.

Oliver and Trisha huddled away from the window as Harold grabbed a wooden chair, hoisting it into the air as if he intended to bash it into them.

"Get out!" Harold shouted, his face red and spit flying from his mouth. "Get out! Get out! Get out!"

"We'll leave," said Trisha. "We're leaving."

No need, the scarecrow replied.

Oliver screamed as the scarecrow's gloved hand reached inside and grabbed his sister.

CHAPTER TWELVE

The scarecrow lifted Trisha high into the air.

Oliver ran outside. He had to act. He didn't have a weapon, so he had to use the closest thing on hand: the broken glass from the window. He grabbed the biggest shard and stabbed it deep into the scarecrow's leg.

Did it feel pain? He had no idea, but his options were limited, so he continued jabbing the scarecrow's leg, over and over and over.

Trisha, meanwhile, screamed and swung her fists at the scarecrow, trying to keep it from biting her. Its mouth wasn't big enough to swallow her whole, but it could probably get the job done in two bites.

The scarecrow didn't bellow in pain, but that didn't mean Oliver wasn't hurting it. He plunged the shard into its pant leg, then dragged it down, tearing open the scarecrow's jeans. Some straw spilled out.

If he could ruin its foot, it might not be able to chase them.

Oliver reached into the rip and grabbed a handful of straw. He pulled it out and threw it onto the ground, then reached for another fistful. The straw was wetter than he would've expected.

His fingers struck something hard.

The scarecrow kicked him with its other foot. Oliver would've preferred a nice soft kick by feet filled with straw, but it was a *real* kick, and it knocked him backward a few steps, leaving the piece of glass in the scarecrow's leg. He fell to the ground and lay there, stunned. But just lying on the ground wasn't really an option, so he forced himself to get back up.

Trisha had been screaming the whole time, but she screamed even louder as the scarecrow swung her at Oliver. The scarecrow was using his sister like a club!

The twins collided. The force of it felt like being struck by a car, and it knocked Oliver back onto the ground, landing hard.

He couldn't breathe.

The scarecrow lifted Trisha into the air again, even higher than before. Oliver didn't think either of them had broken any bones, but with a second impact, they might not be so lucky. He could imagine the scarecrow smashing Trisha into him, both their bodies popping like water balloons.

Though he was in a tremendous amount of pain, Oliver knew he had to fight through it. His and Trisha's lives depended on it! Or, worse, they could be lying there completely broken on the street until they lost consciousness and woke up with hundreds of wires in them.

Oliver got up as the scarecrow swung Trisha at him.

An instant before she would have smashed into him, he stepped out of the way and grabbed her arms. Then he pulled as hard as he could, so hard that he thought he might yank his own arms out of their sockets.

She came free of the scarecrow's grip, and they both fell to the ground.

Trisha wasted no time. She grabbed a big shard of glass from the broken window and stood. Oliver did the same thing.

The scarecrow leaned down toward them. *What are you going to do with those, Oliver? Am I supposed to be scared?*

"Maybe you should be," Trisha told it. It must have asked her the same question.

The scarecrow grinned, showing off its teeth.

There was no escape. The only plan Oliver could think of was for him and Trisha to run in opposite directions so it couldn't eat them both. He supposed they could also try to crawl back in through the broken window and politely ask the man if they could borrow a shotgun, but that seemed unlikely.

Be careful, Oliver. You don't want to cut yourself.

Oliver already had. It was the least of his current concerns.

Why did you have to go and stab me? That wasn't very nice. It wasn't very nice at all. You know what would be more fun? Stab your sister. Stab her right now.

"Shut up," Oliver said.

Go on, Oliver. You've got that nice sharp piece of glass. Use it. Stab her.

Oliver shook his head. "No."

"Is it telling you to stab me?" Trisha asked.

"No." Why had he lied? He'd just blurted out the lie without even thinking.

Stabbing Trisha with the broken glass might be kind of fun. Maybe even more fun than video games. And if he didn't enjoy it...well, it wasn't as if he had to stab her a whole bunch of times. He could just do it once or twice. See if he liked it.

That's right, Oliver. Just try it out. It might be your favorite thing in the whole wide world.

Oliver clenched his fist more tightly around the shard of glass.

"Oliver—?"

He looked over at Trisha, who could obviously tell something was going on. "It's trying to make me stab you!" he said.

As soon as he said that out loud, the desire to hurt his sister vanished.

He slammed the glass into the scarecrow's burlap face, so deep that he lost his grip on the glass and left it embedded in there. Trisha did the same thing. The scarecrow didn't stop grinning as it stood back up to its full height.

A pity. We could've had such a good time tonight.

It reached up and plucked a piece of glass out of its face, then flicked it away. It did the same with the second piece.

My job is to protect this village, so I can't spend the entire night playing with you. You've provided a welcome diversion from the monotony of my existence. Maybe I'll see you tomorrow.

The scarecrow turned and began to walk away.

Oliver and Trisha just stood there, unable to believe their night of horror was finally over. What if Oliver hadn't snapped out of it? What if he had gone after Trisha with the glass? She was the more athletic one, so she would most likely have blocked him and then wrenched it out of his hand, but if she hadn't...

There was no reason to think about that. The scarecrow's attempt to use mind control to trick him into hurting Trisha hadn't worked. And it never would.

Suddenly, the scarecrow spun back toward them. They both let out a quick scream as it grabbed one twin in each hand. Oliver could hear the scarecrow's wicked laughter cackling in his mind as it stood back up and flung him into the air.

He was going to die! He was going to strike the cobblestone road and shatter all his bones. Oliver squeezed his eyes closed and waited for impact. Would he linger in misery for a while, or would everything just go black forever?

He landed sooner than he'd expected, without the stomach-dropping sensation of falling. As he began to roll, he realized the scarecrow had thrown him onto a roof. He opened his eyes and frantically tried to stop himself from rolling, but there was nothing he could grab.

Just as he went over the edge, he wrapped his fingers around the gutter.

The gutter broke most of the way off the side of the house. It bent down, and Oliver plummeted toward the ground. But when he stopped with a jolt, he hadn't yet struck the ground. Then the gutter came the rest of the way off, and Oliver landed with a thud. Though it certainly didn't feel *good*, he wasn't going to die.

He hurriedly looked around for Trisha.

He couldn't see her, but he could see the scarecrow a few houses away, putting more distance between them with each immense stride. Good. The farther, the better.

Oliver wanted to call out for Trisha, but he didn't want to give the scarecrow any reason to come back. He got up, fell back down, got up again, and limped away from the house whose gutter he'd ruined. There were no lights on inside, though they must have heard the commotion. He wondered if a frightened family was huddled inside, praying for him to go away.

Movement to his right.

There she was! Trisha was waving her arms at him. She had also landed on the roof of a house, although she hadn't fallen off. Oliver hurried over.

"Are you okay?" he called up in a hoarse whisper.

"Yeah," she said. "Hurt my arm, but I didn't break anything. I don't know how to get down."

Oliver's tactic of riding the broken gutter down didn't seem like the safest plan. And it wasn't like she could simply jump off and have him catch her. "I'll find a ladder," he told her.

Moving as fast as he could on his injured foot, Oliver went from yard to yard, trying to find one that had a ladder somewhere outside. Though his eyes were fully adjusted, it was still difficult to see in the night.

After searching nine or ten houses, he still hadn't found a ladder, but he did find a house where the backyard was filled with children's toys, including a small trampoline. This would have to do. He dragged it across the yard, hoping the scarecrow didn't decide to come back.

It took so long to get the trampoline to the other house that Oliver started to think the sun might rise first, but he finally dragged it into place.

"You really couldn't find a ladder?" Trisha asked.

"This will be totally safe," Oliver promised. "It's in good condition."

Trisha sighed. She swung her legs over the side of the

roof, very carefully lowered herself as far as she could, then let herself drop onto the trampoline. For a second Oliver thought she was going to land on the springs, but she hit the edge of the mat. She bounced a few times, then safely climbed off.

"How's your arm?" Oliver asked.

Trisha held it up. Even in the dark, Oliver could see it was badly scraped. It looked like it really hurt, and they'd need to make sure it didn't get infected, but she'd live.

"What should we do now?" Trisha asked.

"I thought we were going back to Edith's house."

"That was before the scarecrow attacked. She may not even let us back inside. I think we need to go back to the river and try to find help."

Canoeing down the river at night didn't sound the slightest bit enjoyable, but Trisha was right. They needed to get out of there. They could always wait on the shore for daylight.

"All right," said Oliver.

They made their way through the village. The scarecrow was visible in the distance, walking around, but it didn't seem to be headed their way.

Soon they reached Frank's house, the first house they'd

seen what felt like a thousand years ago. They walked past it and onto the trail.

There was no way they'd be able to navigate this trail without illumination, so they took out their cell phones and turned on the lights. Oliver's battery was at 60 percent. They'd be okay.

As they walked along the trail, Oliver was suddenly very sure that the canoe would be gone. They'd have no way to travel except to wade along the river's edge. Although, if that was what they had to do, they would. Maybe the cold water would make his injured foot feel better.

The bushes rustled right next to them, causing Oliver to almost jump out of his skin. He didn't swing his cell phone over there fast enough to catch a glimpse of what it was, but it obviously wasn't the scarecrow.

When they arrived at the dock, the canoe was where they'd left it. The old rowboat was too.

More bushes began to rustle.

No, it was the *trees* that were moving.

The scarecrow, which seemed to get a thrill out of toying with them, was on its way.

CHAPTER THIRTEEN

Trisha wanted to just leap right into the canoe, but if it tipped over and she plunged into the cold water, she'd deeply regret not taking a few seconds to hold it steady. She crouched and placed her hands on the side of the canoe. "Get in!"

Oliver scrambled in and then braced himself against the dock so it wouldn't tip when Trisha boarded. After she climbed in, Oliver untied them from the dock and pushed off. Then the river's current started to sweep them away.

They'd barely gone a few feet before the scarecrow stepped out into the river before them.

"Paddle! Paddle!" Trisha shouted.

It was already too late. The scarecrow stood in their way.

The twins helplessly moved toward it. Oliver raised his paddle out of the water, preparing to fend off the scarecrow.

It might work!

Oliver swung the paddle like it was a baseball bat. It was a perfect swing, striking the scarecrow directly in the belly. But instead of flying out of the way like something filled with straw, the scarecrow didn't even budge. In fact, the impact hurt Oliver's hands, and he dropped the paddle. Fortunately, it landed in the canoe, and he picked it up again.

The scarecrow held the canoe in place.

"Hit its arm!" Trisha shouted.

Oliver swung the paddle again, striking the scarecrow's arm. It was another perfect swing, and again, it had no effect.

Trisha moved toward the bow. Hitting it with the paddle wasn't helping, but maybe she could pry its hands off the canoe. If they could get free, surely it couldn't follow them down the river, right?

She tried to pry the scarecrow's gloved fingers back, but its hand wouldn't come loose.

Oliver bashed its arm again and again.

The scarecrow, apparently tired of being hit, grabbed

the paddle and yanked it out of Oliver's grip. It tossed the paddle into the water, and the current carried it away.

Oliver tried to help Trisha. Even working together, they couldn't pry the scarecrow's hand off the canoe. How could this thing be so strong? How did it even have muscles?

At least it wasn't speaking to her. Either it was talking to Oliver, or it was too focused on their canoe.

She almost wanted to jump off the side and try to swim again. That was, of course, a terrible idea. They'd be swept away and drown before they went around the next corner. Perhaps if they had time to put on life preservers, they could make it work, yet somehow Trisha suspected the scarecrow wouldn't calmly stand there and let the twins put them on. She didn't want to meet whatever fate the scarecrow had planned for them, but it didn't seem to want to kill them— yet—so that was better than leaping into the cold dark river.

They continued their efforts. The scarecrow wouldn't budge.

Then it grabbed Trisha with its free hand and hoisted her into the air.

"Let her go!" Oliver shouted.

Technically, the scarecrow did as it was asked. But it tossed Trisha back onto the trail. She landed hard, yet not so hard that she heard any of her bones break. For somebody who kept getting thrown around tonight, she'd been remarkably lucky.

She realized she was no longer holding her cell phone. She couldn't remember when she'd dropped it—her phone was either in the canoe or lost forever in the river.

The scarecrow grabbed Oliver. Her brother clawed at it with his fingernails and even tried to bite it, but none of it did any good. It lifted him out of the canoe, then let go of the boat. Trisha watched in anguish as the river current took the canoe away.

The scarecrow carried Oliver as it waded back onto shore. It dropped Oliver next to her.

Enough, the scarecrow said in Trisha's mind. *That's enough.*

It wasn't, though. Trisha refused to give up. The scarecrow hadn't suddenly become friendly. It wasn't going to carry them back to the village, then invite them to roast marshmallows. They had to do whatever they could to get away from it. That didn't mean they should jump into the river, but it *did* mean they should run through the forest.

Trisha glanced at Oliver. "Go!"

The twins got up and ran. Though the scarecrow had the

advantage of a much larger stride, its huge size would make it more difficult to navigate through the trees.

Oliver let out a wince of pain with each step, but he was running surprisingly fast.

Trisha didn't look back. She could hear the scarecrow following them.

Oliver was doing a good job of keeping up with her, so she picked up her pace, and—

She smacked into a large branch.

She was hit *hard*, right in the face, and for one horrifying moment, she thought it might have gotten her in the eye. But as she struck the ground, she realized that, no, she'd just run into it with her forehead. It was too dark to tell if her vision had gone blurry, but she was feeling dizzy and stunned.

Gosh, apparently running through the woods at night was unsafe. Who'd have thought?

Oliver grabbed her hand and pulled her to her feet. She couldn't see anything and was worried that if she ran forward, she'd smack right into that same branch again.

It didn't matter. The scarecrow's hand clamped completely over Trisha's head.

Was it going to try to twist it off or pop it off like the flower of a dandelion?

Don't move, it told her. *Don't make me break your neck. You won't like that.*

Trisha didn't move.

She heard Oliver cry out.

The scarecrow picked up Trisha again. It held her under one of its arms and Oliver under the other, then walked along the path, heading back toward the village. Trisha didn't bother to struggle this time. It was holding her too tightly for her to have any chance of squirming free, and there was no good reason to make it even angrier than it already was.

The only sounds were the scarecrow's steps on the dirt path.

When they reached the edge of the village, it set them down—not gently—on the street.

I'm done with the games. You no longer amuse me. If you try to get away again, I'll squeeze you until your bones pop out.

"What do you want us to do?" Trisha asked.

Sit down.

Trisha and Oliver sat.

Get some sleep if you can. But don't you dare move from this spot.

"We won't, we promise," said Trisha, as if she were being scolded by their parents or a teacher. She was pretty sure she was lying, though. If the scarecrow left them alone, they'd probably try, once again, to flee.

But the scarecrow did not leave them alone. It stood over them, motionless.

After a few minutes, its eyes stopped glowing.

"Is it...is it resting?" asked Oliver.

"I'm not sure."

It seemed really unlikely that the scarecrow would just go to sleep. It wasn't on a pole or anything, so, at the very least, it was awake enough to stand there without falling.

"What should we do?" Trisha whispered.

"I don't know. Nothing we've tried has worked."

Making a sudden run for it seemed like a lost cause. Trisha didn't want to sit there until morning, but she wasn't sure they had a choice.

Oliver lifted his arm, stretching it as far as he could without moving the rest of his body.

The scarecrow's eyes lit up.

When Oliver put his arm back down, its eyes went dark again.

"I think we have to wait here," he said.

Trisha nodded. Though she hated to give up, it was clear that for now, the scarecrow had won. Their only victory was that, apparently, chasing them around was no longer fun for it.

And so they sat. The best thing they could do was get some sleep so they'd be refreshed for whatever challenges awaited them in the morning, but there was absolutely no chance Trisha could fall asleep with the scarecrow looming over them. She might as well try to sleep in a pit of spiders or with a rattlesnake slithering across her bed. She knew Oliver felt the same way.

After a few minutes of silence, Oliver said, "Do you think Dad is okay?"

Trisha started to say, *Of course he is*, but that was ridiculous. Dad was very much *not* okay and might never be okay again. So she settled for saying, "I don't know."

"We'll get him out of there," said Oliver.

"Yeah."

"We won't let them win."

"Uh-huh," said Trisha, without much enthusiasm.

The one plus side to running for their lives from the scarecrow was that the chase had been a distraction from her thoughts about Dad. Now she had plenty of time to think about him. Even if they escaped from Escrow and brought back the police, was it too late? Fifty police officers might kick down the door to the medical center and arrest the mayor and everybody else, but Dad might be beyond saving. Who knew what those wires actually did?

"Do you have your phone?" Trisha asked.

"No. I lost it when the scarecrow pulled me out of the canoe."

Of course. It was perfectly in line with the way everything was going that they both had lost their cell phones. Their phones were really just glorified flashlights around here, but now if they managed to escape, they'd have to find actual people, not just a signal.

Had Dad been aware of them looking into his room? Did he know that she and Oliver had failed to rescue him?

Enough. They had enough problems without Trisha making up this scenario where Dad was disappointed in them. If anything, he'd be proud of them, even if their efforts so far hadn't amounted to anything.

Oliver reached out his arm again. The scarecrow's eyes started to glow.

"Stop that," said Trisha.

Oliver lowered his arm. "Just testing."

"You already tested."

"I was testing again."

"It can hear us, you know."

"I know." Oliver was quiet for a moment. "Should we try to sleep in shifts? You could take the first one."

"You could sleep?"

"I don't think so. We could try, though. I may not be able to sleep, but I know I'm going to go insane if I have to just sit here for the rest of the night."

"You try," said Trisha. "I'll keep watch."

Oliver lay on the ground and curled up on his side, hugging his knees to his chest.

Trisha tried to come up with a plan for how they were going to get out of this.

Nothing came to mind.

Well, except to separate. The scarecrow couldn't chase after both of them at once. If Oliver kept it distracted in the village, she might be able to get back down to the river. The big obvious problem was that she didn't know what the scarecrow would do to her brother if she escaped. Would it stick with whatever it was planning to do to the twins, or would it tear him apart, limb by limb, out of anger?

They couldn't risk it. And she really didn't want them to split up anyway. They'd stick together, no matter what.

As she sat there, she tried to remind herself of happier

trips. Trips on the river where the canoe *hadn't* overturned, leaving them trapped in a village by a giant living scarecrow. There'd been plenty of them. Still, try as she might, Trisha couldn't distract herself from thoughts about the trip where they were forced to eat too much ice cream.

Oliver kept shifting positions. Normally, he slept like he was dead, except for the snoring, so trying to fall asleep on the ground beneath the scarecrow obviously wasn't working out for him.

Trisha waited and waited. She had no idea what time it was or how many hours remained until the sun rose.

Oliver sat up.

"Did you get any sleep?" Trisha asked.

"No. Do you want to try?"

"No."

They sat there waiting for daylight. Trisha began to wonder if the sun would ever rise. Maybe they were now trapped in a land of eternal darkness.

Finally, though, the sky began to lighten.

The scarecrow, giving absolutely no warning, reached down and picked them both up. They didn't even bother screaming or trying to get free. The scarecrow carried them down the street, making great time with its long legs, until it reached the village square. It dropped them onto the ground, then leaned against its pole just as the first beam of sunlight shone over the horizon.

Now what? Was this a chance to flee? It couldn't be that easy.

Trisha could see the fronts of one row of houses, and all the doors began to open, as if the people who lived in them had been standing there with their hands on the doorknobs, waiting for sunrise. They left their homes and walked toward the village square.

A door slammed shut. The twins glanced in that direction and saw both Mayor Clancy and Belinda storming toward them, having just emerged from the medical center.

Lots and lots of people were walking toward them. None of them looked happy.

CHAPTER FOURTEEN

Trisha and Oliver stood there as the angry mayor walked over to them. He glared at them but said nothing as more and more people walked toward the village square.

Was it going to be all 999 of them? It was sure starting to appear that way. Trisha looked around for a sympathetic face and saw none. One man was smiling, but it was a cruel smile, like he knew something awful was going to happen to them and couldn't wait for the fun to get started.

It only took a few minutes for what Trisha assumed was the entire population of the village to gather. They stood quietly, staring at the twins. From the looks Oliver and Trisha were getting, she worried the mayor might blow a whistle and turn the villagers loose to rip them to shreds.

Mayor Clancy gestured to a very thin man, who handed him a megaphone.

"Citizens of Escrow," he said. "Thank you for being here today. I know you have jobs to do and lives to live, but sometimes we all have to gather as a community. Sometimes it's for celebration, and sometimes it's not. As you already know, this time it's the latter."

The mayor pointed at the twins. "Yesterday, these children arrived in our village. They didn't come with torches or guns, but they were invaders nevertheless. We treated them with nothing but kindness. We gave their injured father treatment. We gave them a free lunch at Agatha's Café, with dessert! We gave them a safe place to stay for the night. We even let them bask in the presence of the scarecrow! But did they appreciate it?"

"No!" several different people shouted. There were dozens of shaking heads.

"That's right, they didn't!" the mayor shouted. He was so loud, Trisha didn't think he even needed the megaphone. "They disrespected Agatha's fine meal! They snuck out of

Edith's home in the middle of the night! And, worst of all, they ridiculed the scarecrow!"

Should they argue? Would anybody listen?

"That's not true!" said Trisha. "It's not true at all! We didn't make fun of the scarecrow."

"Frank?" asked the mayor.

Frank pushed his way through the crowd and walked up to the mayor, who held the megaphone out for him. "They said it was creepy," Frank announced.

"That's not *ridiculing* it!" Trisha insisted.

"I'm afraid we'll have to agree to disagree," said the mayor. "Just like you probably think it's perfectly fine to let a delicious dessert go to waste. Thank you, Frank. You can go now."

Frank stepped a few feet away.

"We live here because we want no part of what's out there! Yet we did everything we could to help these ungrateful, entitled children, and they spat in our faces every step of the way. But do you know who we have to thank for stopping them?"

"The scarecrow!" somebody shouted. Dozens—no, hundreds more people shouted the same thing.

"That's right, the scarecrow! Once again, he protected

our fine village. Can you imagine the destruction these little demons would have caused if they brought more of the outside world right to our front doors? Who knows how many intruders would be wandering our streets right now, getting into our business? But try as they might, these rotten, poorly raised children were no match for the scarecrow!"

Everybody cheered. The mayor smiled for a moment but then waved his hands for silence. He looked over at the scarecrow. "But it's exactly as I feared." He walked over to the scarecrow and touched its leg, running his fingers over the cuts in the overalls where Oliver had stabbed it with the glass. "They've damaged it."

The people in the crowd made various sounds of anger. Trisha was pretty sure she heard somebody actually growl.

"They ripped his face as well! Maliciously tried to tear apart the being who keeps us safe."

Trisha wanted to explain that when a giant scarecrow is chasing you, you fight back. But she knew the crowd—which was starting to feel very much like an angry mob—wouldn't listen.

"But try as they might, they haven't damaged it beyond repair! Everybody bow your heads."

The citizens all lowered their heads. Six women, all

wearing black dresses, walked over to the scarecrow in single file while somebody Trisha couldn't see played what she thought was a clarinet. It was a somber tune, like they were at a funeral.

The two women at the end of the line were carrying a ladder, which they leaned against the scarecrow's pole. They climbed it as the other women began to sew up the rips in the scarecrow's clothing.

Trisha knew she was probably supposed to lower her head as well, but this whole thing was really strange, and she didn't want to be caught off guard. She watched the ceremony. It wasn't as if she could get in worse trouble.

The women on the ladder sewed up the gashes in the scarecrow's face. They worked quickly and were done within a couple of minutes. They climbed back down as the other women finished. They formed a line again and walked away. The clarinet music stopped.

Everybody looked up again.

"Let us all give thanks to the scarecrow for keeping us safe," said Mayor Clancy.

"Thank you," said everybody in the crowd, speaking in a group whisper.

"And now we must deal with the unpleasant business at

hand. Most unpleasant indeed. I assure you, it gives me no pleasure to think about executing anybody, much less these children of such a tender young age."

Trisha felt like she'd been punched in the stomach. *Executed?* Oliver looked horrified as well.

The mayor chuckled. "You should've seen your faces." He raised his voice and spoke to the rest of the crowd. "Did everybody see their faces?"

Many of the villagers laughed. Not like they were watching a comedy movie—there was a definite *meanness* to their amusement.

"Only the scarecrow is allowed to put somebody to death. You'll survive your punishment, but you may wish you hadn't."

"You can't punish us," said Trisha. "We haven't done anything wrong!"

"Well, I'm afraid what you're saying isn't quite accurate, young lady. I'm sure you thought we were going to throw a party in your honor and shower you with gifts. Maybe hire a clown to make balloon animals and entertain everybody. But, no, everybody here knows the decision we have to make isn't whether or not to punish you because that decision has already been made. It's how we're going to do it."

"Just let us go," said Oliver. "We won't tell anybody about this place."

"Oh, really? You'll leave your daddy behind? Doesn't make you a very good son, does it? No, young man, we won't be letting you go today or any day. What we need to do is figure out how merciful to be."

"No mercy!" somebody shouted.

"Now, now, now, none of that," said Mayor Clancy. "This is going to be an orderly and respectful process. There are a few factors to consider. They aren't even teenagers yet, so perhaps we could simply lock them in our prison for a very, very long time."

Trisha wanted to cry.

"Yet what kind of message would we be sending if we let them off that easy? How would we be dissuading future criminals? What would stop somebody else from deciding it was perfectly okay to cut up the one who watches over us?"

The paced back and forth as he shouted into his megaphone. "This is a democracy, and we're going to go with whatever the majority decides. And if you want to let these wretched children off easy, that's how you should vote. But if it were up to me, we'd set an example. We'd make them suffer. We'd make their punishment something this village could talk about for years to come. You know what I'm talking about!"

"The Hills!" Frank shouted.

"You're darn right, the Hills! It's a harsh punishment but a fitting one. Show of hands, who votes for the Hills?"

Trisha couldn't say for sure that every single hand went up, but she couldn't see any that *weren't* up. What were the Hills? Why would everybody want them to receive an even worse punishment than a prison sentence? It seemed impossible that the villagers of Escrow could be so sadistic.

Unless this was all one big hilarious joke. But by now it was clear that the people in the village were deadly serious.

"Then it's settled!" said the mayor. "Thank you all for understanding that sometimes we need to send a message, even if it's to ourselves."

"I want a chance to talk!" Trisha demanded.

"We've heard enough from you already," said the mayor.

"Tell everybody what you did with our dad!"

"Yeah!" shouted Oliver. "You've got our dad locked up with a million wires stuck in him! You act like you're trying to help him, but you're not! I bet the people here would love to know what you're doing in the medical center!"

The mayor lowered his megaphone. "That's not anybody's concern."

"He's hiding stuff from you!" Trisha told the crowd. "Make him show you what he did to our dad!"

"Enough," said the mayor. "Keep talking and you'll regret it."

"How could things get any worse for us?" Oliver asked. "Tell the people what you're hiding from them!"

"I said that's enough!"

"Tell them!"

"Tell us!" said Frank. "Tell us what you're hiding!"

Then Frank burst out laughing.

The mayor chuckled as well. He raised the megaphone to his mouth again. "Uh-oh," he said. "Looks like we've been caught. They know my secret." He gestured to the crowd. "They know *our* secret."

There was laughter throughout the crowd. Trisha's small glimmer of hope that they might get out of this mess faded.

"You're right," he told Trisha and Oliver. "I wasn't being honest with you. But everybody else knows the true story, so I'm afraid you haven't done yourself any favors."

CHAPTER FIFTEEN

"The scarecrow gives far more than it takes," said the mayor. "The price for its protection is small, but there *is* a price. When the scarecrow gets hungry, we must feed it."

The people in the crowd nodded.

"We don't get many visitors, and we get fewer still that we can make disappear without the outside world poking its nose into our business. So it's usually one of us who has to make the ultimate sacrifice for the rest of the village's safety. Denise Grove. Percy Morgan. Carver Young. Those are just three who volunteered to do what needed to be done. And we appreciate their sacrifice more than they'll ever know."

The mayor pointed to a woman standing near the front of the crowd. "In fact, there's Bonnie Young right there. Your husband was a great man. A brave man. He didn't cry, and he barely even screamed. It's because of men like him that the village of Escrow is one of the safest places to live in the entire world!"

The crowd applauded. Oliver couldn't believe they were so upbeat when they were about to condemn a couple of kids to a horrific punishment. They'd all looked really angry when they marched out here, but now the mayor and the rest of the crowd looked almost giddy.

"Yet sometimes you're presented with a gift, one where you can't believe your good fortune. A gift like a lost pair of twins showing up at your village with their injured daddy. Nobody knows they're here. Their daddy is unconscious, so all you have to do is wheel him right inside and start hooking him up. The scarecrow gets hungry when there are more than nine hundred and ninety-nine people in Escrow, and it likes a special...*flavor* to its meal. Those wires are making your daddy all nice and tasty."

Oliver's legs buckled beneath him, and he dropped to his knees. Trisha took his hand and helped him back up.

"That's right, we're keeping your daddy alive and

delicious for when his time comes. Mmm-mmm good! I'm half tempted to try a piece myself!"

Everybody in the crowd laughed.

"Now, now, don't get all upset," Mayor Clancy told the twins. "I'm only kidding. What tastes scrumptious to the scarecrow would taste foul to a human, so I promise I won't take a single bite out of your daddy."

The crowd laughed again. They seemed to be having a great time.

"You two will be locked away until the next feast, whenever that turns out to be. Could be weeks. Could be years. Now, we do need to plant evidence from you and your daddy far from here so nobody shows up on our doorstep looking for you. The outside world loves to identify people through their dental records, so those teeth of yours are pretty darn valuable!"

They should run. They'd never get away, not from the hundreds of people, but they should at least try, right?

"Enough jibber jabber," said the mayor. "Let's take these kids to the Hills!"

The crowd surged forward. They lifted Oliver and Trisha into the air and carried the twins like they were crowd-surfing at a rock concert. The crowd of hundreds of people moved down the street, as if this were a great big celebration.

Oliver couldn't really keep track of time while he was being jostled around and carried by the crowd, but it might have been about fifteen minutes before they arrived at their destination. The crowd put them back on the ground, not particularly gently but definitely with more care than the scarecrow had used.

They stood in front of a barn. It had one big door in front, which was currently closed. There were no hills that Oliver could see.

"We haven't had to do this in...I don't even remember how long," said Mayor Clancy. "Do you remember?" he asked the man who'd handed him the megaphone.

The man shrugged. "A decade, maybe?"

"A decade." The mayor smiled at Trisha and Oliver. "Back before you two could walk, probably. When do kids learn to walk? When they're two years old, right? I don't know. It doesn't matter. Anyway, we haven't taken anybody to the Hills in a long time, but we keep it good and ready, just in case! Who wants to do the honors?"

A few dozen people raised their hands.

"All right, Frank. You were the first to meet them when

they invaded our village, so you can show them their fate. Now, don't anybody else go and ruin the surprise!"

Frank went to the barn door and started to open it.

"Not so fast!" said the mayor. "Don't just swing it wide open. Draw out the suspense. Make them wonder."

Frank closed the door again, then opened it with excruciating slowness. The mayor shook his head with annoyance.

"That's too slow. This isn't that hard, Frank. Somebody else do it. Bonnie, you do it!"

Frank, hanging his head, walked away. The widow Bonnie took his place and, slowly but not too slowly, opened the barn door.

Trisha saw what was inside before Oliver did. She gasped.

Inside were several huge dirt hills, tall enough to reach Oliver's waist. They looked very much like...ant mounds.

He really didn't like where this seemed to be headed.

"Welcome to the Hills!" said the mayor, gesturing grandly to the barn. "You may have noticed that wooden barrel over in the corner there. Young man, you can read, right?"

"Yes," said Oliver.

"Then why don't you read what it says on that barrel?"

"Honey."

"Very good, very good. That's exactly what it says. Are you starting to put the pieces together?"

Oliver was, and he didn't like it at all.

"See those two metal poles coming up out of the ground?" asked the mayor. "There's one for each of you. Go on and have a seat next to one. Lean right up against it."

Oliver wondered what would happen if he refused. He knew it would end with him leaning against the pole anyway, so he might as well save his energy. Trisha seemed to realize the same thing. The twins walked into the barn and sat against the poles.

The man who'd handed the mayor his megaphone crouched behind Oliver. "Give me your hands."

Oliver held out his hands. The man cuffed them together. Then he did the same thing to Trisha.

"All right, Frank, I'm going to give you another chance," said the mayor. "You know what to do."

Frank walked over to the corner and picked up the barrel.

"Did you know that honey never goes bad?" asked the mayor. "It's true. They've found honey with the mummies of ancient Egyptian pharaohs, and you could still spread it on your biscuit. It's never too late to learn new things."

"Even if you'll be dead soon," said Frank.

"Less talking, more pouring," said the mayor. "We've already said that these poor criminals will survive the experience. But our prison is reasonably comfortable, even the part hidden away from outsiders. Being covered with fire ant stings would make it quite a bit less comfy, don't you think? Don't worry—we'll get you out of there before they finish you off. Probably."

Frank turned a knob over the spout, then held the barrel over Trisha. For a few moments, nothing came out, and then a very thin trickle of honey poured out of the barrel and went into Trisha's hair. She recoiled.

"Ladies and gentlemen, this won't be a fast process," the mayor told the crowd. "But you knew that already. We're just going to keep on pouring the honey until these two criminals are good and covered, and then we're going to let nature run its course. You can get back to your daily routines, or you can hang around here for as long as you want."

About half the crowd dispersed, with people moving closer to take the places of those who'd left. There still wasn't much honey in Trisha's hair, but it was coming out faster now.

When her hair was dripping, Frank switched over to

Oliver. He cringed as the honey got in his hair. A thick trickle of it went down the back of his neck.

Thus far, no ants had emerged from the dirt hills.

Honey was running down Oliver's face. Frank switched back to Trisha, pouring honey all over her shirt.

"You don't have to worry about getting shortchanged on this experience," said the mayor. "Those ants will crawl right under your clothes."

People started to get bored and leave, but there was still a very large crowd of spectators as Frank covered the twins with honey. It was getting everywhere, and even without the looming threat of receiving hundreds of ant stings, this would have been a miserable experience.

"I think that's good," the mayor finally said. "We don't want them to drown in that stuff. Drowning's an awful way to go, but it's not as bad as ant stings."

"Do you want me to kick one of the hills?" asked Frank.

The mayor shook his head. "Nah. Those insects will figure out what's going on soon enough."

Oliver and Trisha just sat there, covered in sticky honey. At least Oliver wasn't thinking about his foot. Although as soon as he thought, *At least I'm not thinking about my foot*, he was reminded of it, and it began to ache again.

"You two don't have to be quiet," the mayor said. "You can cry, or beg for mercy, or talk to each other about what you should've done differently. Just sitting there isn't entertaining anybody."

"How about I tell you that you're a terrible mayor?" asked Trisha.

"Well, if you did that, I'd have to say that you're a bit young to judge a quality mayor, and your opinion wouldn't mean a lot."

"Then what if I told you that you were bad at punishment?"

"Am I?"

"Yeah."

"Is that because you've somehow picked the lock on your handcuffs? Are you gonna jump up and fight your way through all these people?"

Oliver glanced over at her hands. He'd be really, really, really happy if Trisha had picked the lock on her handcuffs. But she hadn't. Oliver had hoped that the honey on his wrists might make them slippery enough for him to yank his hands out, but if anything, it would be harder to get out now.

"Nope," said Trisha. "But we're twelve years old."

"Right."

"And we're not crying. We're not begging for mercy. To me, that means you're bad at your job, because if you can't make a twelve-year-old girl cry when you're going to cover her with ants, you're doing something wrong."

The mayor grinned. "Now, now, it's irrelevant that you're a girl. Girls can handle as much pain as boys. More, actually. I suppose you're trying to fluster me and make me angry enough to make a mistake, but I honestly admire your defiance. I'd like to believe I'd act the same way in your shoes."

"You wouldn't," said Trisha. "You'd be crying and begging for mercy."

Somebody in the crowd laughed.

The mayor spun around. "Who was that?"

Nobody said anything.

"You'd better fess up before I have a few more poles brought in here! I'll bring in enough for everybody! *Who was that?*"

A few people pointed to an old man in a brown hat. "I'm sorry," he said. "It was an accident."

"An accident? You were accidentally amused?"

"I coughed."

"I know the difference between a laugh and a cough. I should shove your head into one of these anthills right now.

Get out of here. I don't expect to see you again until I've forgotten what you look like."

The old man hurriedly left the crowd. The mayor turned back to the twins.

"Well, congratulations, young lady! You made me mad! Are you proud of yourself?"

Trisha said nothing.

"What you *didn't* do is make me mad enough to make a mistake. So, Frank, why don't you go ahead and give those anthills a gentle kick?"

Frank walked over to the hill that was closest to Oliver.

"Not too hard now. Don't destroy their home. Just let them know there's a treat for them waiting outside."

Frank gently tapped the anthill with his shoe. Then he went around tapping the others.

By the time he stepped back out of the barn, red ants were pouring out of the hills.

And they quickly crawled toward the honey.

CHAPTER SIXTEEN

Now Trisha kind of wanted to cry and plead for mercy.

A long line of ants crawled toward her. She couldn't get away from the pole, but she was otherwise free to move around, so she scooted herself up into a standing position. Oliver noticed what she was doing and did the same thing.

"Good, good," said Mayor Clancy. "Don't make it too easy for them. We've got plenty of time for them to completely overwhelm you."

Under normal circumstances, Trisha wasn't afraid of ants. Spiders, yes. She hated spiders. Ants didn't bother her at all...unless there were thousands of them crawling toward her. And these were red ants, probably fire ants, whose stings were incredibly painful. They weren't called *fire* ants because of their color; it was because their stings burned like fire.

She hated to harm living creatures, but she was fully prepared to stomp on as many of these ants as she could.

The ants kept coming. So many of them. One line of them headed for Trisha, and another headed for Oliver. They got to Oliver first, and he frantically began to step on them.

"You're off to a good start," said the mayor. "The question is how long can you keep it up? You have to sleep sometime."

The ants reached Trisha, and she stomped them as well.

Another line of ants had formed. It wasn't clear yet if it was coming for Trisha or her brother.

Soon there were several lines of ants crawling toward them. It wasn't difficult to keep stomping on them yet, but Trisha knew it was going to get harder and harder.

"Oooh, be careful!" said the mayor. "One almost got you!"

Trisha ignored him. There were now so many ants coming for them that she and Oliver had to be constantly stomping, like they were doing a weird dance.

Ants were now crawling on top of her shoes.

She felt one crawl on the back of her foot.

That one stung her. She tried not to make a sound—she

didn't want to give the spectators any satisfaction. She stayed quiet, but this was only the first sting. How silent could she be as she was getting stung for the second, third, hundredth, thousandth, millionth time?

"Look at her face!" said the mayor. "She definitely got stung!"

Oliver winced as he received his first sting.

"Stop!" shouted somebody from the back of the crowd. "That's enough!" Was that Belinda? It sounded like her, but Trisha was too busy stomping ants to pay attention.

The mayor ignored the shouter.

"I said 'stop!'"

Trisha looked at the crowd. Somebody was pushing their way through. Yes, it was Belinda wearing a white lab coat.

A couple of ants stung Trisha while she was distracted.

Belinda walked up to the front of the barn. "Let them go," she told the mayor. "They're just children."

"They're rotten children."

"I told you to let them go."

"I'm sorry, are you the mayor now? What makes you think you have any say in what happens here?"

Belinda reached into her pocket and took out a scalpel.

Trisha watched the conflict but made sure to pay attention to the countless ants swarming all around her.

"What are you going to do with that tiny little thing?" Mayor Clancy asked.

Belinda waved the scalpel in the air. "Whatever it takes."

"You think you can fight off all of us?"

"No. But I know where to cut. The first one of you who comes at me is going to do a lot of bleeding. Do any of you care enough about what happens to these kids to die over it?"

Nobody in the crowd moved toward her.

"Do *you* care enough about what happens to these kids to die over it?" the mayor asked her. "The best-case scenario for you is to get banished, but we both know it will be much worse than that. You were one of the most respected members of this community, and you threw it all away for these children. What's wrong with you?"

"That's not your problem," said Belinda. "I said to let the kids go. Now!"

Trisha continued to frantically stomp on the ants. They were all over her pants now.

"No," said the mayor. "We won't be doing that. You can wave your little toy knife around all you want, but it's not going to change anything."

Belinda stepped into the barn and held the blade of the

scalpel against Oliver's throat. "What if I ended it early, then? Ruined everybody's fun?"

"Don't do that," said the mayor.

Oliver froze. He couldn't move around with a scalpel to his throat, and Trisha could see he had ants all over his clothes.

"I hope you're taking me seriously," said Belinda. "I have nothing to lose."

"Fine!" said the mayor. "Unlock the handcuffs."

"Do the girl first," said Belinda.

The man who'd locked them up carefully stepped into the barn, looking like he really didn't want to be in there with all the ants. He quickly crouched and unlocked Trisha's handcuffs. She immediately moved toward Oliver.

"No!" shouted Belinda, pointing the scalpel at her. "You're safe! Don't spoil this!"

The man was clearly even less enthused about going over to Oliver, but he did it. A moment later, the handcuffs fell away. Trisha and Oliver hurried out of the barn and began brushing the ants off themselves, which was almost impossible with all the honey.

Belinda dropped the scalpel.

"Are you happy with yourself?" the mayor asked. "You know you're just going to take their place, right?"

Belinda suddenly looked confused. "That wasn't me."

"I beg your pardon?"

"That wasn't me."

"Of course it was you. We all saw it."

Belinda shook her head. She sounded like she'd just been woken out of a sound sleep. "I don't care what you do to these kids. I would've been happy to pour the honey on them. The scarecrow made me do this."

"The scarecrow?"

"Yes. It wanted me to stop it."

"That lie won't get you out of this," said the mayor.

Trisha and Oliver continued wiping the ants and honey off themselves. Trisha wished Belinda had insisted upon them being sprayed down with a hose before she dropped the scalpel.

"I'm not lying, I swear!" said Belinda, sounding frantic. "It was the scarecrow! It was the scarecrow! It was the scarecrow!"

"That's absurd," said the mayor.

"It's not absurd," said Trisha. "The scarecrow talked to us too. It gets into your mind!"

"I know that. How could I be mayor of this village without knowing that? The scarecrow talks to me every day. What I don't get is why it would try to spare these little monsters."

"I have no idea, but it did," Belinda insisted. "Why would I make that up? Why would I throw everything away to save them? It doesn't make any sense. It doesn't make any sense at all. The scarecrow wanted them out of the Hills, and it made me do its bidding!"

"I bet she's lying," said Frank.

Mayor Clancy chewed on his upper lip, lost in thought. "She's right," he said. "She'd have no reason to do this. If anything, she'd have more reason to want to see them punished."

"But—"

"Do you want to defy the scarecrow?" the mayor asked Frank. "Do you want me to tell him you're the reason we put those kids back in the barn against its wishes?"

"No."

"Then you have no reason to contribute to this conversation. If Belinda was lying, we can bring the kids right back here. The ants aren't going anywhere. I don't know about you, but I'd rather waste some time going back to the village square than ignore Belinda and find out she was telling the truth."

They all walked back down the street. This time the crowd seemed very ill at ease, far from the celebratory mood they'd been in on the way over. Trisha was pretty sure most of them would rather return to their homes and not be part of whatever was going to happen next. One man did step away from the crowd, then seemed to think better of it and joined them again.

Trisha and Oliver weren't carried this time. As they walked, they tried to help each other get rid of the ants they'd missed. Trisha had several painful stings, but at least her entire body wasn't covered with them. In the overall picture of how bad things were for her right now, a few ant stings were no big deal. She'd be very relieved when she was no longer covered with honey.

"Are we saved?" Oliver asked.

Trisha shrugged. They were better off than they had been a few minutes ago, but she assumed they were a long way from being saved. They hadn't exactly become friends with the scarecrow last night. She couldn't think of any reason it would want to spare them their grisly fate.

By the time they made it back to the village square,

Trisha was pretty sure she and Oliver had gotten rid of most of the ants.

The scarecrow was where they'd left it.

"We're back," Mayor Clancy announced.

He frowned.

"Right, right," he said, looking up at the scarecrow. "I didn't mean to offend you. It just seemed like the polite thing to say."

The mayor nodded vigorously. He looked incredibly nervous. "Yes. Of course. Yes. I completely understand. Yes. Yes. You get why we chose that, right? I'm sorry. I'm sorry. Yes."

The mayor took a deep breath. He reached for his megaphone, but the man who carried it wasn't next to him, so he shouted instead. "Ladies and gentlemen, I take full responsibility, but the scarecrow is angry with us. We chose poorly."

What did that mean? Did it want Trisha and Oliver to meet a worse fate, or did it want them to be set free?

"Sending them to the Hills seemed like the right choice," said the mayor, "but it wasn't horrible enough."

Trisha's mouth dropped open. Not *horrible* enough?

"The scarecrow thought we would choose a fate worthy

of these children. We did not. *I* did not. We have until sunset to come up with a method of justice that satisfies the scarecrow." The mayor coughed and cleared his throat. "That is all."

CHAPTER SEVENTEEN

"What could be worse than ants?" a woman asked.

The mayor gaped at her. "Are you out of your mind? You're questioning the scarecrow?"

The woman put her hand over her mouth in horror. "I'm sorry. I wasn't thinking."

"Of course you weren't thinking! That's completely obvious! Unless you have something useful to contribute, stop talking!" The mayor looked up at the scarecrow as if to apologize. Then he turned his attention to the people in the crowd. "What could we do that's worse?"

A man up front raised his hand. "Maybe make them eat the ants?"

"What?"

"Ant stings would hurt worse on the inside, right?"

"No! That's a terrible idea! Think before you speak, people! The scarecrow is already angry with us. Come up with some good ideas."

A little girl, maybe eight years old, raised her hand. Oliver hadn't even noticed other children besides the boy in the house. Were these adults really going to let her watch other kids get swarmed by fire ants?

The little girl's mother held her other hand. She leaned down, and the girl whispered something into her ear. "*Oh*," the mother said, looking shocked. She stood back up straight. "I'm not sure I feel comfortable sharing this."

"Share it," said the mayor.

The woman shared it. It was, without a doubt, the most horrific thing Oliver had heard in his entire life. There were several gasps from the crowd. There was something very deeply wrong with this little girl, and Oliver hoped she would get the psychological care she so desperately needed.

"That's...pretty bad," said the mayor. He turned to the scarecrow. "Would that suffice?"

He waited for a long moment.

"What did he say?" Belinda asked.

"Nothing."

"Nothing?"

"Did I mumble? He didn't say anything!"

"Should we go ahead and do it?"

"No, we shouldn't do it! We'll wait for the scarecrow to approve! What other ideas does everyone have? Let's hear it!"

People kept making suggestions. Many of the suggestions were positively nightmarish. After each one, the mayor would pause, but the scarecrow hadn't responded. Was it waiting for the right suggestion before it bothered to reply? Nobody knew.

After a while, Oliver stopped listening. He was past being scared. He was more focused on the maddening itching of the ant stings and the honey drying on his skin in the summer sun. He'd give anything for a hot shower. At least his foot was feeling better.

"What do we do?" Belinda asked. "If it's not saying anything, shouldn't we just pick the most awful thing we've heard so far?"

"We can't undo that," said Mayor Clancy. "What if the scarecrow is unhappy with the method we choose? What are we going to do, wait for them to regrow their arms?"

"No, but shouldn't we do *something*?"

"He will talk to us when the time is right."

By lunchtime, the scarecrow still hadn't communicated with anybody. The lucky people were seated on the benches, while everybody else, including Oliver and Trisha, sat on the ground.

Agatha wheeled out a cart piled high with cheese sandwiches for everybody. She didn't offer any to Oliver and Trisha, and they knew better than to ask. Oliver wasn't hungry anyway.

After lunch, nobody said much of anything. They just sat around, waiting for something to happen.

The day stretched on and on. Everybody was completely miserable, although Oliver was confident he and Trisha were the most miserable, even if you disregarded the honey.

Around dinnertime, Agatha returned with another cart of cheese sandwiches. "Couldn't you at least have used a different kind of cheese?" the mayor asked.

"I wasn't prepared to feed half the village."

Once again, Oliver and Trisha weren't given anything.

"The sun is going to set soon," said Belinda.

"We can all see that," the mayor told her.

"What do we do? We're not supposed to be outside after dark. Not ever."

"I don't know. I just don't know." The mayor ran his hand over his bald head. He looked up at the scarecrow. "I'm begging you for an answer. We'll do whatever you want. We just need to know what that is."

He sighed with exasperation. "He's not speaking. These are unusual circumstances, so we're going to have to make our best guess. I think he wants the children to himself when the sun sets."

"We can't leave them out here," said Belinda. "They'll run away."

"You're going to stay with them."

"I most certainly am not!"

"You have to," said the mayor. "What if the scarecrow starts talking again? There'll be nobody to answer."

"Then you do it!"

"I have to be around to lead these people. The scarecrow spoke to you before. It has to be you."

Belinda looked like she wanted to cry. "Please don't make me."

"I'm sorry," said the mayor, not looking sorry at all. He once again reached for a megaphone that wasn't there. He shouted, "Everybody, return to your homes. If you're needed, you'll get a call. Otherwise, try to have a restful night."

The crowd wasted no time in dispersing.

The mayor pointed at Oliver, his finger an inch from Oliver's nose. "Don't cause any problems. I'm warning you."

"Or what? You'll cover me in honey and feed me to ants?"

"I've given you the warning. What happens next is up to you." The mayor walked away.

Soon the twins were alone with Belinda.

"Everything will be fine," said Belinda. It seemed she was saying it to herself, not Oliver and Trisha. "Everything will be completely fine." She sounded like she wanted to follow that with a shriek.

The sun was setting.

The three of them watched it silently until the sun disappeared below the horizon.

The scarecrow's eyes glowed.

Belinda jerked her head toward it so rapidly, it was like she'd been slapped.

"What?" she asked. A tear trickled down her cheek. "No, please don't say that. I didn't fail you. It wasn't my fault. I didn't decide any of that. It was the mayor."

She backed away from the scarecrow.

"It wasn't me!" she insisted. "Don't be mad at me! I didn't do anything wrong! I know you protect us! I know we should have done a better job serving justice! But it wasn't my fault! It wasn't me! Please! You have to believe me! Look in my heart! Can't you see what's in my heart? None of this was my fault! I'm begging you to believe me!"

Oliver wasn't sure what the scarecrow said to her after that, but it couldn't have been good, because Belinda let out a scream that made his ears ring. Then she turned and ran.

The scarecrow stepped forward. It reached down and grabbed her. It picked her up, held her right in front of its face, and grinned.

Oliver thought it was going to pop her into its mouth, but the scarecrow instead spun around, working up some momentum, and then flung her into the air, far higher than it had thrown Oliver and Trisha the previous night.

Belinda sailed over the nearest building, screaming the entire way.

Then her scream abruptly stopped.

The scarecrow turned back toward the twins.

Hello, Oliver. Are you ready for the worst night of your life?

"Leave us alone!" Oliver shouted, as if that would do any good.

Oh, no. There's too much fun to be had. I think you and your sister should fight.

"Maybe you should..." He couldn't remember what he meant to say.

But the scarecrow was absolutely right. Fighting with Trisha felt like the right thing to do. She thought she was so much better than him, but he'd prove her wrong. Everything that had happened since the river rapids was her fault, all of it, every little bit, and she needed to pay.

They argued all the time, but they'd never actually gotten into a physical fight. Well, they'd fought over toys when they were younger, and there was that one time when she'd tried to pull him out of the recliner because she wanted to sit there. Stuff like that.

Oliver clenched his fists.

Trisha realized something was wrong. "Oliver...?"

Oliver took a swing at her. She mostly moved out of the way. His fist grazed the edge of her nose, but it didn't seem to hurt.

Who did she think she was, dodging his punch?

Oliver couldn't remember ever being so angry.

"Oliver, stop it!" Trisha said. "The scarecrow is doing this to you!"

"You blame the scarecrow for everything! Maybe we should listen to what it has to say! Did you ever think of that?"

Instead of using his fists, Oliver curled his fingers into claws. He was going to rip his sister apart and laugh the whole time he did it.

She slapped him across the face, really hard.

For a split second, he realized he didn't want to do this.

Yes, you do, Oliver. She's your enemy.

Oh, yes, he wanted to do this. And then he could live here. He could live with the happy villagers and never have to leave the scarecrow again.

Did he really want that?

Trisha tried to slap him again, but he grabbed her wrist.

The first slap had done something.

She was his twin sister! Why would he want to hurt her? That was madness!

They were supposed to have a much closer bond than normal siblings! They were supposed to be the best of friends! They were supposed to be inseparable!

Oliver slapped himself in the face as hard as he could.

He let go of Trisha's wrist.

Then he slapped himself a few more times, just to be sure.

Stop that, said the scarecrow.

"Shut up," Oliver told it. "I'm not listening to you any-more. Go back to your field, loser!"

All right, then. I suppose we're done playing.

The scarecrow grabbed Oliver with both hands. It lifted him to its mouth, which was open wide, incredibly wide, wide enough to fit a twelve-year-old boy inside. And then it shoved him in.

CHAPTER EIGHTEEN

Trisha screamed as the scarecrow crammed her brother into its mouth. Oliver kicked his legs as he struggled to get free, but he was already halfway gone.

She rushed over to the scarecrow and kicked its legs as hard as she could, trying to divert its attention to her instead.

Oliver screamed, although his screams were muffled by the hay inside the scarecrow. He kept waiting for the scarecrow's sharklike teeth to come down upon his waist, biting him in half.

The scarecrow pushed him in farther. Oliver's body bent forward, head down. There was no place for him to go. One more shove, and Oliver was completely inside the scarecrow's mouth. Did it have a throat?

It closed its jaws, casting him into complete darkness.

Trisha kicked the scarecrow as it swallowed her brother whole.

The scarecrow didn't seem to care until it gazed down at her.

Yummy.

Oliver slid down inside the scarecrow, which felt like wet, slimy straw. The smell was worse than anything he'd experienced in his life. Far worse than the time he'd forgotten to take out the garbage before a two-week vacation. He didn't know what death and decay smelled like, but the stench in here was *rotten.*

He desperately longed for the time in his life when his

worst problem was getting in trouble for forgetting to take out the garbage.

Was her brother alive? Dead?

Trisha didn't know how the inside of the scarecrow's body worked. Did it have guts? Did it have digestive juices?

She needed to get Oliver out of that scarecrow, but how? She couldn't tear it open with her bare hands. Belinda had dropped her scalpel all the way back at the Hills.

Agatha's Café wasn't that far. It would have knives.

She ran.

Oliver was now completely upside down. He hadn't thought he was claustrophobic, but it felt like the scarecrow was tightening around him. Maybe it was.

He tried to call for help—not that it would do any good. Trisha was aware of his predicament, and when he opened his mouth, wet straw slithered into it.

So he screamed with anger and frustration inside his mind instead.

Trisha sprinted under the scarecrow's legs, hoping she could confuse it and gain a few extra seconds. Her speed was one advantage she had. It wasn't *much* of an advantage, but she'd take what she could get right now.

Wait! What was that ahead?

The red, white, and blue spinning pole of a barbershop!

It was closer than Agatha's Café, and it would have scissors. Since she hadn't noticed a hardware store, this was her best bet. She ran toward it.

Oliver could barely breathe.

And his skin was starting to burn.

He could feel the scarecrow lumbering forward. They were moving. He didn't know if that was good or bad...

Trisha knew the scarecrow was gaining on her, but she was far enough ahead that it couldn't catch her with a single step.

Or so she hoped.

Its foot landed behind her, close enough to make her push faster but not close enough to flatten her. Running all those drills at practice was paying off. She felt another surge of adrenaline.

She switched directions, veering off to the right. From what she'd seen, the scarecrow was fast, but it wasn't very graceful. If she kept zigzagging, it might not be able to catch her.

Of course, she was losing precious seconds to save her brother. She needed her strategy to work.

Oliver refused to give up. He could barely move, it was hard to breathe, and the scarecrow's stomach acids, or whatever, were starting to make his skin hurt. But he wasn't going to die inside this thing. Not a chance.

He reenacted the combat moves he used to win his video games. Sure, he was mostly wiggling in the tight space, but maybe he could give the scarecrow a bellyache.

Trisha reached the barbershop's glass storefront. She jiggled the doorknob. It was locked. She kicked the glass as hard as she could. It didn't break.

She glanced over her shoulder. The scarecrow was close. It started to reach for her. She didn't have time for another kick. Instead, she ran between its legs again.

Stand still.

Did she hear frustration in its voice? She really hoped so.

Oliver continued to struggle. Being upside down, the blood was rushing to his head, making him feel woozy. But he couldn't pass out. He had to stay awake. Had to stay alive.

Trisha crossed back to the barbershop. She considered smashing into it at full speed, but being sliced to ribbons would not help her brother. So she kicked again.

The entire glass storefront did not come crashing down,

which would've been nice, but the glass did break, leaving a hole that she could *almost* safely squeeze through. She didn't have time to make it bigger, so she ducked and went through the hole, hoping she wouldn't cut herself too badly.

Oliver really hoped Trisha would save Dad. He hoped Trisha, Dad, and Mom all knew how much he loved them. He was going to miss them. He was going to miss his friends at home, his teachers. He was even going to miss homework...

Trisha found a light switch and turned it on. Inside, the barbershop was neat and clean. There were no scissors or combs on the counter in front of the barber chair, so Trisha flung open the drawer in the workstation and found something. It wasn't a very big pair of scissors, but it would have to do. She didn't have much time.

Trisha whirled around at the sound of glass shattering. The scarecrow's hand punched through the storefront, and it crawled into the barbershop after Trisha.

Suddenly, Oliver wasn't upside down anymore. He bumped from side to side. What was going on out there?

Trisha backed away from the scarecrow. She knocked into a tray that clattered like silverware dropped into the dishwasher after dinner. She looked down. On the tray was a straight razor, the kind that gave a really close shave. That would probably work better than the scissors. She picked it up and held it in front of her, trying to appear intimidating.

Do you really think that scares me?

The scarecrow climbed farther into the shop. Its back scraped against the ceiling.

Trisha's heart raced. To her horror, she was being backed into a corner. There was no way to escape.

Ready to join your brother?

Oliver wondered what would happen if he bit down on the straw. It was already filling his mouth. He'd been focusing more on the fact that he could barely breathe than the fact that biting the scarecrow's insides might hurt it.

He chomped down.

Then he spat out the wet straw. It smeared on his face in the tight space. He bit again.

The scarecrow twitched.

Its expression flashed with distress before it grinned at Trisha.

Then it had another instant of distress.

Trisha didn't know what was going on with the scarecrow, but she was going to take advantage of the distraction. She lunged forward and slashed at its face with the straight razor.

Oliver could feel the scarecrow flinching as he bit it from within. He could barely move his head, but he kept biting as vigorously as he could manage.

Trisha slashed at the scarecrow's burlap face, making contact underneath its right eye. The fabric ripped to the left corner of its mouth. Then she slashed again down the center.

A large flap of its face fell away.

Trisha screamed at the glistening skull underneath.

Had Oliver heard Trisha scream? He wasn't sure.

The scarecrow was moving.

And Oliver was upside down again.

The scarecrow crawled out of the barbershop. Trisha was filled with relief, but no! Oliver was still inside. She had to believe he was still alive. She had to get him out. She hurried outside after it.

The scarecrow stood to its full towering height. Its giant skull reflected the moonlight.

Trisha heard angry-sounding gibberish in her mind. It was the scarecrow's voice, but in a language she'd never heard.

Somehow, the scarecrow looked even more frightening than before.

There was no time to waste. She ran at it.

It slammed its foot to the ground, missing her by inches and making the street quake. Clearly, it was enraged.

She ran under its legs again.

The scarecrow wasn't going to make it easy for her. But its arms seemed to be in proportion to a human's arms, which meant there might be a place on its back it couldn't quite reach, like when she had a really bad itch.

To get to it, she'd have to climb the scarecrow. She was ready.

She put the straight razor between her teeth, hoping very much that it didn't slip, and then grabbed the back of the scarecrow's pant leg.

It shouted more gibberish in her mind.

It had been a while since she'd done any real climbing, but when she was eight or nine, Trisha used to climb the tree beside their house all the time. The tree, of course, was not moving and trying to swat her off. But the scarecrow's clothing was baggy, making it easy to grab a handhold, and she pulled herself up its leg without *too* much trouble.

Trisha saw its hand coming toward her and leaped to its other leg. She almost lost her grip and fell to the ground, but adrenaline was pumping through her body. She was moving like a superhero. She kept climbing, hoping it couldn't reach her. She'd know soon enough if it could.

Trisha heard some extremely unfriendly English words along with the gibberish.

She'd have to let go with one hand to use the razor, but she could hang on, no problem. She took the razor out of her mouth and slashed down the scarecrow's back, cutting as deeply as she could.

This wasn't going to work. There might very well have been a spot on the scarecrow's back that it couldn't reach, but she was bigger than that spot! She'd have to scrunch up and make a smaller target.

She tucked in her legs and tried to squeeze herself into a ball. It wasn't easy, but since there was now a slash in the back of the scarecrow's shirt, she had something to wedge her feet into.

The scarecrow seemed to be thrashing around wildly. What was happening out there?

Trisha slashed again, making the opening even bigger. Then she pushed her legs into its back, squeezing between the straw and its clothing. She'd cut this thing wide open from the inside.

She slashed away, tossing straw into the air as she worked. The straw was moist and disgusting.

"Oliver!" she shouted. "Where are you?"

He could hear Trisha! He couldn't tell what she was saying, but that was definitely her voice.

With renewed enthusiasm, he began to shout. He was badly muffled, but he hoped it was enough.

Oliver was alive! She could hear him, just barely, but it was his voice.

She continued to slash away, now completely underneath the scarecrow's clothing. Then her blade hit something hard and stuck.

His sister was getting closer. He was going to survive!

Oliver was getting louder and louder. Trisha continued to fling handfuls of straw out of the scarecrow, trying to reach him—and figure out what she had hit. It was a bone. A giant rib.

She thrust her hand downward, digging as deeply as she could, and touched Oliver's shoe! Or the shoe of somebody else the scarecrow had eaten. But it was almost definitely a shoe!

She threw more and more handfuls of straw out of the scarecrow's body, freeing his legs.

Trisha was completely covered in slime, which made it slippery to grab his ankle, but she pulled.

Oliver started to slide free. Finally, she could see his head. He gasped for breath.

If she could keep this up, maybe they could destroy the entire scarecrow.

No.

It grabbed her, swung her around in front of its ruined face, and began to squeeze.

CHAPTER NINETEEN

The scarecrow squeezed Trisha until she thought her whole body was going to burst like a water balloon. Then it loosened its grip.

It started talking in gibberish. But then it said: *No. Too easy.*

Oliver pushed his way out of the wet straw and found himself dangling out of the scarecrow's back. He was exhausted, but there was no time to rest. He wasn't sure what happened to Trisha, but he could hear her yelling. She was in danger!

He tried to scramble down the scarecrow's leg, but the straw was slippery, and he slid. He didn't fall *that* far, and he didn't land on his head. Right now he was enjoying the little victories.

The scarecrow twisted with Trisha in its grasp. Its blank stare chilled Oliver.

Oliver forced himself to get up. His legs were shaky from his fall, but he sprinted toward the one place where he thought he might defeat the scarecrow.

Then he tripped and fell.

Trisha slashed at the scarecrow's hand, hoping it would let her go. She'd worry about the fall to the street later.

The scarecrow didn't budge. Instead, it raised its foot to stomp Oliver flat.

"Don't!" Trisha shouted. "Let me do it!"

The scarecrow froze. *What?*

It was difficult for the scarecrow to convey confusion with its burlap in tatters and its skull peeking out, but that was exactly what it did. And then it seemed to realize that confusion was her intention. That its hesitation had given her brother a few seconds to escape.

Oliver ran.

Trisha had no doubt he had a plan—to save himself *and* to help her.

The scarecrow growled in frustration and went after him.

As Oliver ran from the scarecrow, he tried to keep as close to the buildings as possible, hoping they provided a little protection. Many of the businesses had awnings, so maybe it made it harder to see him from the scarecrow's height. Any coverage was useful. Not that he was safe yet. Not at all.

He reached Agatha's Café and kicked his throbbing foot at the front window. It probably wouldn't break, but—

The window shattered as if he'd set off a bomb next to it. With no real crime in Escrow, maybe they didn't need good windows on their stores.

Oliver ran into the restaurant.

The scarecrow crouched in front of the café. Through the front window, Trisha saw Oliver flip on a light switch, then push through the swinging door to the kitchen.

What was his plan?

The scarecrow reached into the café with its free hand, overturning tables and chairs. Then it smashed its fist into the ceiling, shaking the entire building.

The floor trembled as if there were an earthquake. Oliver slid his hand along the counter as he hurried to the stove.

It was an electric stove, not gas. Still, he could work with that. He turned on all four of the burners.

The building shook again.

The scarecrow swung its free hand around the inside the café. Debris flew everywhere. A large piece of plaster struck Trisha in the head.

Make him come out.

Nope, Trisha wasn't about to help the scarecrow. Sorry,

not sorry. She knew the scarecrow could crush her in its fist at any time, so she hoped whatever Oliver was doing would help her break free—and fast. Before the scarecrow got any angrier.

The burners glowed red. Oliver grabbed an apron and tossed it onto the stove. Then he found a pair of towels and tossed them on too. What else? He started to take off his shirt, but it was covered in goo, and he couldn't risk it not burning properly. He found a hairnet and added it to the pile. It would have to do.

Now he just needed them to catch on fire.

The ceiling of the café split in half as the scarecrow pushed farther into the building. Trisha struggled to shield her head in its grip.

Why wasn't the fabric catching fire? Oliver had made popcorn once, and it'd caught on fire in the microwave by accident. Now, in a life-or-death situation, he couldn't get a cloth apron and some towels to catch fire on a hot burner!

He squinted at the pile. Maybe there was a little bit of smoke...

The swinging door burst off its hinges, flying across the room and almost hitting him.

The scarecrow slithered toward him, with Trisha still in its grasp. Its face had been slashed open, revealing a...no, that was too scary to look at. Oliver needed to focus on the burners.

"C'mon! C'mon, catch fire!" he urged under his breath.

Trisha saw what her brother was doing. "Hurry!" she shouted.

The apron finally caught fire. It wasn't much of a flame, but it was something.

Oliver snatched up the fabric with a pair of tongs and flung it at the scarecrow.

It fluttered to the ground a few feet short.

He really wished he had a flamethrower, like in one of his video games. This place didn't seem fancy enough to have one of those mini blowtorches he'd seen on cooking shows.

He ran forward and scooped up the apron. The scarecrow grabbed for him. He tossed the apron on its hand.

It recoiled, and Trisha broke free of its other hand.

The twins rushed back into the kitchen. Now both towels were on fire. So was the hairnet, but it had already almost completely disintegrated. They each picked up a towel by the corner and returned to the dining area.

They had to get closer.

Oliver danced around, waving the burning towel. He needed the scarecrow's undivided attention, so he sang, "Burning towel! Burning towel! I've got a burning towel!"

Trisha took that opportunity to rush closer and toss her own towel on its back.

Gooey straw didn't burn well, but the scarecrow's clothing did.

The scarecrow sat upright, bashing its skull against the

ceiling so hard that a couple of bone chips fell to the floor along with ceiling fragments.

Oliver tossed his towel onto the scarecrow's chest.

It grabbed the towel and flung it away, but its shirt was already burning.

The scarecrow frantically scooted backward.

Was it enough? Would the fire stop the scarecrow? What was the most flammable item in a restaurant kitchen?

"Flour!" shouted Trisha, as if reading his mind. "Find a bag of flour!"

She was right. Oliver couldn't remember where they'd learned about dust explosions—probably from a TV show—but flour was incredibly flammable if you scattered it into the air!

It didn't take long to find. The bag was huge—so big that they needed to lift it together to haul it into the dining area.

The scarecrow had withdrawn to the street, batting at the flames while on its knees.

The twins rushed outside. They couldn't let it get away!

Oliver tore open the bag, and then he and Trisha flung the contents at the scarecrow.

The cloud of flour burst into flames with a loud *whoomph*.

The scarecrow spun around, completely aflame.

It let out a wail so loud in Oliver's mind that he covered his ears. The scarecrow staggered back. It waved its flaming gloves and arms, and the crackling grew as loud as the scarecrow's screams.

It staggered toward the twins. The breeze blew bits of burning straw, so it looked like it was raining lit matches. Oliver and Trisha screamed and ran in opposite directions as the scarecrow teetered, then dove at them.

The gigantic burning monster crashed onto the street.

It missed them.

Trisha and Oliver stood there, watching silently as the unmoving scarecrow continued to burn. Through the flames, Trisha glimpsed what looked like bones. One of its large button eyes fell off and rolled a few feet before toppling over.

Trisha rushed over to Oliver and gave him a big hug.

"I can't hear it anymore," said Oliver.

"Me neither. It's gone." Trisha pulled away, which wasn't easy because their clothes stuck together. "You're really gross," she said.

Oliver raised his eyebrows. "Uh, wait till you see a mirror. So are you."

Trisha let out a short laugh, but there wasn't time to

celebrate. They still had to get Dad and get out of the village.

As they hurried away from the burning scarecrow and debris, lights began to turn on in the surrounding homes. People stepped outside, their mouths gaping at the scene before them.

"It's safe," Trisha told them. "You can come out. It can't torment you anymore. You're free."

"What have you done?" the mayor shrieked, running toward them.

"We saved you all," said Oliver. "The scarecrow was controlling you. It tried to control us too. But it's over now. It's dead."

"What have you done?" the mayor repeated. "What have you done? No, no, no, no, no. You don't understand. You don't *understand*. It was *protecting* us!"

Oliver didn't try to argue. He was too relieved—and focused on getting to his dad.

The mayor paced back and forth. "This is bad. This is so, so bad."

In the distance, a woman screamed.

Then another.

The mayor looked up at the sky. His mouth fell open. "Oh, no..."

Oliver followed his gaze. In the darkness there was a motion in the air. He heard rustling...flapping?

The breeze intensified, and the clouds shifted.

A large shadow flew past the moon. Then the night plunged back into darkness.

"What is that?" he asked.

The mayor just stared at the sky in terror.

"What *is* that?" Oliver asked again.

"The crows."

CHAPTER TWENTY

A crow swooped down and landed in front of the mayor.

It wasn't a typical crow. Not even close.

It was larger than a human. Its bloodred beak was jagged, like teeth. Dark liquid dripped from its wings. Its talons were sharp and curved like the Grim Reaper's scythe. Its feet had gnarled claws—too many of them, at least six or seven on each foot.

The monstrous crow let out a deranged squawk that made Trisha's ears ring. Its long black tongue protruded from its beak as it did so.

Trisha absolutely, positively could not believe her eyes. Everything about this town had been utterly bizarre, but *this*...

The crow flapped its wings, rising a couple of feet into the air. Then, moving almost too fast to see, it flew past Trisha, Oliver, and the mayor. It snatched up a woman in its feet and flew high into the air. In two blinks of an eye, they were both out of sight.

More crows flew in from the surrounding woods, then took to the sky, carrying their screaming victims with them.

Trisha and Oliver ran. The mayor followed close behind.

The scarecrow lay motionless on the street. The fire was almost out, leaving behind a giant charred skeleton.

"Stop!" somebody shouted behind them. It sounded like Frank, but Trisha couldn't be sure with all the noise around them.

"You don't get to run!"

It was indeed Frank. Trisha turned to shout back, but he continued, "You stay right here and face the—"

A crow swooped down, then carried him into the air.

The twins continued running. They needed to find shelter.

All around them, crows were carrying people away. One giant bird sat on somebody's roof, tearing off pieces of wood with its beak.

"The medical center!" said Trisha. "It's secure!"

"Where do you think I was headed?" the mayor snapped.

They reached the door to the medical center. The mayor stuck his hand into his pocket, vigorously digging around for his keys.

"Hurry!" said Oliver.

"I am hurrying! And what makes you think I'm letting you in there with me?"

A crow flew past them, carrying an old man who was hitting the bird with his cane.

"Where's it taking them?" asked Trisha.

The mayor finally found his keys. "I don't know. We hoped to never find out!"

A crow landed in the street a few feet from them.

"Stay away from me!" the mayor yelled.

Another crow landed at their side. It let out a ghastly squawk.

The mayor began to blubber. "Please...please...leave me alone! I didn't do anything wrong!"

The first crow leaned forward and clamped its beak on the mayor's ankle, then rose into the air, taking the mayor with it.

Trisha watched in horror as the mayor dangled upside

down. They couldn't let those things carry him away, could they?

The second crow took flight and grabbed the mayor's arm in its beak. He screamed in pain. The two birds tugged on their prey, each trying to claim the mayor for themselves.

Trisha, against her better judgment, rushed forward to help. She waved her arms at the crows, trying to scare them off.

Instead, they flew away, the mayor dangling between them.

Oliver gasped and slapped his hand over his mouth as he watched.

"This is horrible!" said Trisha.

"I know! Did you see that?" Oliver looked queasy.

"No, I mean he took the keys with him!"

With a light rustling sound, a crow landed on the cobblestone next to them. Then another. Then a third. A fourth. A fifth.

Trisha and Oliver joined trembling hands. If this was the end, they were going to go down fighting.

One of the crows took a step closer. It tilted its head, almost quizzically, then let out a chirp. The other crows chirped as well, looking at each other as if having a very serious discussion.

Then the first crow flew off, and the others followed.

Trisha and Oliver hurried away from the medical center and returned to Agatha's Café, which seemed like their safest option, as long as the entire place didn't crash down upon them.

They sat on the floor and waited silently. They could hear a lot of screaming, both close and distant.

After a while—a very long while—the screams stopped.

They kept waiting.

"Did you know you're all red?" Trisha finally asked.

Oliver looked at his arm. "Scarecrow stomach acid, I guess."

"Does it hurt?"

"A little. I'll live."

Trisha didn't think she'd fallen asleep, but daylight spilled into the café sooner than she would have expected, so maybe she had.

A few citizens were walking around, looking scared and stunned. Apparently, the crows hadn't carried away all 999 residents. Trisha wondered how many were left.

"How are we going to get in to see Dad?" she asked.

"I know where there's another key," said Oliver. "Wait here, and I'll go get it."

"Where is it? I'll come with you."

Oliver shook his head. "Belinda probably had one. We don't both need to see that."

"Oh."

"So I'll go."

Trisha decided to let him. Oliver came back a short while later with the key. He didn't share any details, and Trisha didn't ask.

Oliver unlocked the door, and they walked down the spiral hallway until they reached their father's room. Peering through the small window to make sure he was alone, Trisha saw he looked like he was sleeping peacefully.

The twins rushed in and wrapped him in hugs. "It's going to be okay, Dad," said Trisha. Dad didn't respond.

"There really isn't much to this equipment," said Oliver. "Should I turn it off?"

"What if it's keeping him alive?"

"I think it's what's putting the...*flavor* in him."

"Yeah, turn it off," said Trisha.

Oliver flipped the switch. A soft hum they hadn't noticed

before stopped. Then there was a loud hiss, like the brakes of a bus.

"I don't *think* we did anything bad," said Oliver.

Trisha searched the room, looking for something to cut the wires. Bingo. She found a pair of wire cutters in a drawer.

She started cutting the wires where they connected to the machine, hoping this would be safer for Dad. Some liquid dribbled out of them, but it was blue, not red. There were a lot of wires, but the cutters made it easy, and she was done in a couple of minutes.

They'd worry about getting the wires out of Dad when they found a real hospital. For now, they needed to get him out of the building.

There was a gurney against the wall, presumably the same one used to carry him here. They rolled the gurney over to his bed, and then, being extremely careful, Trisha and Oliver moved Dad from the bed onto the gurney, grunting with the effort. They piled the wires on his chest and then wheeled him back through the hallway.

They pushed him down the street and past the scarecrow's bones.

They passed a few townspeople. Nobody tried to stop

or even acknowledge them. They stared vacantly like zombies.

Trisha and Oliver made it to the trail that led out of the village. Belinda had mentioned a shortcut, but they weren't about to risk getting lost in the woods to look for it.

They were careful as they pushed Dad along the trail, yet they still made surprisingly good time. There were some difficult spots, but they never dropped him off the gurney.

When they reached the dock, Trisha felt a great sense of relief. Their journey wasn't over, but the worst had to be behind them.

They approached the rowboat, and Oliver dropped their supplies onto the bench seat. It promptly sank. Okay. Perhaps the worst wasn't behind them. At this point, all Trisha could do was laugh.

Pushing Dad along the shore would be much more challenging than floating downriver. But they could do it. After everything they'd been through, they could do anything.

It was more difficult than Trisha expected, even with adrenaline blasting through her veins. The shoreline was rocky and uneven. This was going to take forever.

Well...as long as it didn't *literally* take forever, they'd be fine.

As they rounded the first corner, Oliver pointed ahead. "Whoa! Look at that!"

"What?"

"There!"

It was their canoe. It had washed up on shore. Trisha couldn't believe their good fortune, even though they were long overdue for a little good luck.

They got Dad into the canoe and climbed in after him. They didn't have phones, supplies, or a paddle, but they were alive. They floated away, leaving Escrow behind them.

About an hour into their journey, Dad opened his eyes. He sat up, leaned over the side of the canoe, and had a huge coughing fit.

"What's...what's...?"

"Shhhh," said Trisha. "Relax. We'll explain everything."

"What are—?"

"We promise we'll explain everything later, Dad. Get some rest," Oliver added.

He went back to sleep. Oliver and Trisha just floated down the river in silence for a few minutes. Trisha felt a deep sense of relief, but she didn't feel safe. Not yet.

Oliver broke the silence. "Thanks for cutting me out of the scarecrow."

"Thanks for saving me those other times."

"I guess twins make a pretty good team."

Trisha nodded. "I guess we do."

"Do you think you'll ever want a hot fudge sundae again?"

"Are you kidding? I could go for a jumbo hot fudge sundae right now! Not really, but they aren't going to ruin dessert for me. Or canoe trips."

Dad woke up a little later, groggy and confused. "What happened to me?" he asked. "What are all these wires?"

"It's a long story," said Trisha. "But you'll be okay."

"Are you two all right?"

"Yeah. We are."

"Why is Oliver all red?"

"Sunburn," said Oliver.

"Where are we?"

"I'm not sure," said Trisha. "But we're bound to find help soon."

"Does your mother know where we are?"

"Not yet."

Dad ran his fingers along the wires. "I have a million questions."

"We'll answer as many as we can. Later. Right now, just relax."

"I feel like maybe we shouldn't tell your mother the whole story. You know, if we want to take another trip ever again."

Trisha and Oliver smiled. They couldn't agree more.

ACKNOWLEDGMENTS

Thanks to Tod Clark, Donna Fitzpatrick, Jamie LaChance, Michael McBride, Jim Morey, Bridgett Nelson, Annette Pollert-Morgan, and Paul Synuria II for their creepy assistance with this book!

ABOUT THE AUTHOR

Jeff Strand has written a bunch of books, most of them scary ones. He is reasonably confident that he could outrun a giant scarecrow should the need arise, but hopes not to have to test that out. He loves haunted houses and licorice, and is no fan of tomatoes.

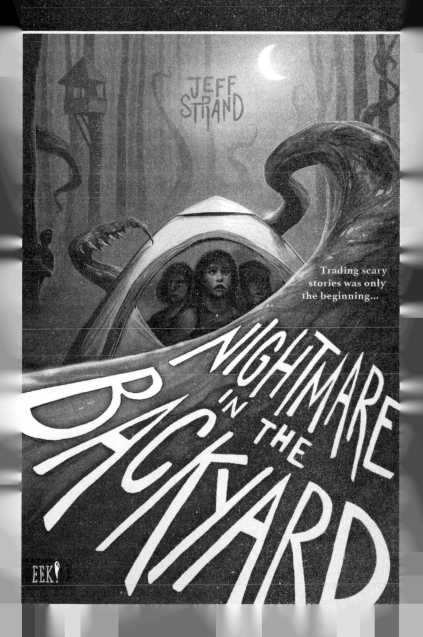

JEFF STRAND

Trading scary
stories was only
the beginning...

NIGHTMARE IN THE BACKYARD

EEK!